Half Burnt Cigarette and a Little Love Note

Our Choices Make Our Destiny

Vandita Mishra

notionpress
.com

INDIA • SINGAPORE • MALAYSIA

Notion Press

Old No. 38, New No. 6
McNichols Road, Chetpet
Chennai - 600 031

First Published by Notion Press 2018

ISBN 978-93-86295-90-3

For the ones who fail to give up!

PREFACE

In the present day, we are all in a hurry, we want everything quick. For instance the same knowledge which came after devoting a lot of time with the books has now come to our finger tips, the same things which were acquired after years of hard work become a necessity as soon as one starts earning money! And unfortunately the same trend has taken over love as well and the same love which was nurtured slowly with time now sees it's high and low peaks within a year or maybe two. We are modern and so are our emotions and so is our love!

Half burnt cigarette and a little love note evolved by my everyday observations of this changing trend in love and relationships! I have spoken to people, discussed their problems, heard stories of the unknowns and I had just one conclusion to make which was that in the haste in which we lead our lives today, we probably do not know as to where we are truly heading!

There is much more to the book than just relationships. It's a narrative that takes you through the journey of a married woman and at the same time awakens you about much smaller and bigger concerns existing in our society. It shows you the realities that a woman faces in her life. It takes you to the corners of India where the huge debates on woman equality and education are still unheard of. A blend of some seriousness and some thrill, this book is set across two different cities, Lucknow and Hyderabad and it will make you live through two different cultures of India. It's a narrative with which you will be able connect at some point or the other and at the end there will be a lot that you will take back from it. Thank you for picking up my book, and welcome to my world.

Vandita!

ACKNOWLEDGMENTS

First of all, my heartfelt thanks to my readers who picked this book to read. It's you who will make me write more and write better.

I couldn't have completed this book without the motivation and inputs from my strongest pillar, Parijat. I fall short of words for this man for having heard everything that I had to say with a patient ear. Even if it was after his night duties, he was wide awake and completely attentive and gave the best critique to my text.

I thank my friend Mahesh for lending me his time and for uplifting my spirits in dull times.

I thank my parents who have always let me live the way I want to and who have always supported me in whatever I do. The book was kept a secret from them until of course, it came in the process of publication. And of course, I can't forget to thank my brother Rajeev for answering my millions of questions with regard to the book from time to time.

Team Notion press has been very helpful throughout the process of publication, you guys are extremely professional and your inputs were extremely valuable.

PROLOGUE

While everyone around me was dancing with joy, while my parents were tensed that things should go just fine, while my sister was advising me on the make-up for my big day, while I was preparing myself to be the bride, I got a call from him. "Hey, where is the venue? I am at the airport," he said. My heart started beating a little faster, what was he doing in my city? I never wanted him to attend my wedding, I thought. "What, why, where?" I uttered some bizarre words in that confused state of mind. "I am just kidding, I am at work," he said. The thumping heart allayed down, and the hollowness crept in again, I wanted him to be around and did not want him to be around at the same time. "It's your big day tomorrow, all I want to say is that you are the best and there is just no doubt about that. Please don't change after you get married. I know you will have certain responsibilities and obligations but please be there for me whenever I need you." "I don't know what makes you even say that but just because you have asked for it; I promise that I will always be there for you, no matter in which state of mind I am or regardless of where I am at that point of time." "Thanks, you made my day!" He said.

While the make-up artist moved her brush over my face and applied kohl to my eyes the next day, I thought how different my life was now than what I had imagined it to be like. While I draped myself in my wedding dress and had a final look at myself in the mirror, I thought, how different was the feeling on this day than what I thought it would be like. While once I was always full of energy and positivity, now I just sat in low spirit and negativity. I thought about my graduation days, I thought how Sahil and I used to be and had planned to be, I thought about my ambitions, my dreams, I thought about Akash. It's funny how sometimes our life takes some unalarmed turns which changes us and everything around us forever.

CHAPTER 1

I had double checked on the cleanliness of the house, had my breakfast well, spoken to my mom, spoken to a friend and had checked my Facebook account many times since the morning. And yes, I was supposed to wash some clothes I remembered, but then for some reason there was no water in the tank. I had put a complaint but the taps were still dry. Meanwhile, on the radio, some lady was talking about women multi-tasking nowadays! I knew even I could be really good at it but then, I should have had some tasks to do!

I was back in Lucknow and jobless once again; I remembered the same phase two years back when I got frustrated with the internal politics in the dental institutes and went to work in Hyderabad city. But this time it was different; this time I had resigned and come because I was married here; my husband was here and my house was here. We had been allotted a small two-room flat in the medical college campus, where my husband was a resident. I remember when I had first seen that flat it was in a really bad state, there was leakage of water from some places on the roof, big black ants had occupied all the corners of the floor, while some horrid looking lizards crawled on most of the walls; I had tried opening a window to get some fresh air but the entire panel had fallen down. I wasn't expecting a bungalow of course, but our flat didn't even have the basics right. We had put a lot of efforts into fixing everything, got some pest control done, got it painted well and kept it as nicely as we could, to make it a cozy little house.

It was all quiet and green around our flat, and of course, so was the entire residential portion of the campus. Contrary to the hustle and bustle that was going on just a kilometer away in the hospital, where Sahil, my husband was, here I was in the middle of all quiets, with locks on the doors of the adjacent flats, watching the trees and squirrels around and thinking what I could do next. Technically it had been two and a half months since I was married, but my married life had begun after I actually shifted with Sahil just a fortnight back. Day in and day out the only thoughts that were hovering in my mind were those of the changes that had happened in my life over the past two years, and how they had multiplied and turned me into a very different person! Things are so unpredictable aren't they?

CHAPTER 2

Sahil's schedule was packed! He did have a fixed time to leave the house which was early morning at 7.30 am. But there was no certain time for him to return. Four days in a month he was away for night duties, he did not have any days off either. Woof! I don't know what he felt like to be in one of the busiest branches of the medical fraternity, but yes certainly it was way too difficult for me. I used to see him running around the house and getting ready in the morning, after which I used to crave for him to return back, which was never before my dinner time. He had a master's degree in paediatrics and was now working as a resident to refine his skills and learn more about children who were less than one month of age, neonates is what they call them. The branch he was in itself required a lot of dedication and hard work. Sahil wasn't bothered about no days off or about being busy because he always wanted to get into this field. I could see that passion in his eyes to do the best for his patients. He wasn't bothered regarding me complaining about his busy schedules either, because he always wanted to marry me, and I could see that passion in his eyes to do the best for me as well.

I had known him for eight exact years before we got married; we were good friends, very good in fact. It was because of him that I had pursued my ambitions, he supported me in whatever I did; by the way, I specialized in treating children's teeth, Pedodontist is what they call me in my field. Sahil had been a constant support for me over the years, people had come and left, things had changed, but Sahil was all the same and always with me despite anything that had happened in my life over the eight years that I had known him.

It was during summer a couple of years back when I had first met him with a few other friends of mine. Graduation days! Aren't we so different when we are graduating? We try to impress people, try to link some boy with some girl and of course try to make relationships and get marriages done in our own head. Our gang was no less. Sahil was a cousin of my friend, Vilosha. It was during a casual visit to her hometown when I had first met him. We were pursuing our graduation then. While I was studying in Lucknow city, he was based in a city nearby which was around 200 kms from Lucknow. We were in the parallel batches and were expecting to graduate in the same year. Thus Vilosha got eager to make a plan with Sahil and his other friends so that we could all have a good time together over dinner. I, Vilosha and our gang were the future dental girls and Sahil and his friends were the medicine boys. I was never bothered about who was who; I used to be a "content in my books" kind of a person, but of course your friends never let you be the serious way especially when you are a teenager or while you are in your early twenties. “Wow Vaani, he would suit you the best,” said Archana, one of my friends who was with us that day. “Blaa who cares,” I said. But least did I expect that the little teasing which followed that night would take all the possible turns and get us to being a married couple one day. Even after we got back to Vilosha’s place, the little leg pulling and teasing continued, as to how me and Sahil would be in future, how Vilosha’s house would be one of my in-laws house, and how I will have Vilosha turning from a friend into a relative and so on and so forth. I laughed it off that time, but I think it did affect me somewhere. So much so that surprisingly I found myself blushing and could not resist silently copying Sahil’s number from Vilosha’s phone that night.

CHAPTER 3

"I usually don't message or call people this late at night..." pop went my message to Sahil, it was around eleven thirty at night. Those are the days when scholar Vaani used to be in a strict schedule; got up at six-thirty in the morning and slept at eleven in the night kinds. "Ok," was the blunt reply which I got, however. "Good luck for your exam tomorrow, I got a distinction in general pathology last year, I am sure even you will manage well." I messaged again with a hope to extend the chat, "Thanks, will try! Goodnight," was what I got next to end the conversation. Basically, I was a little excited ever since I had met him; who doesn't like such phases, when all you feel is some dancing butterflies in your stomach and some thrill of the unknown in your mind. But Sahil was probably someone who didn't like such feelings, he was more cautious, reserved and balanced.

His exams got over a week later from then, and one day while I was washing some utensils in my hostel, I got a call. The name on my phone splashed as Sahil, and my heartbeat went totally up. I left my work halfway, ran and locked myself in my room to get secluded from the boarder's disturbances and received the call. "Hey Sahil," I said as soon as I answered, "I hope your exams went all well," "Oh yes," he said, "All good, the results are awaited anytime soon. Next year they will be taking us to the general ward as well, we will start observing patients and we will start reading medicine and surgery." "Great," I said. "We are already exposed to working on the patients, I did my first cavity filling yesterday but I hope it doesn't come out anytime soon" I laughed. "Oh don't worry about all that, you are there to learn, do your best and leave the rest," he assured me. He was always very motivating types, someone with whom you could share anything and everything, someone with whom you could be totally yourself. I was in a world of mine own and blushing and dreaming while I was talking to him. It was then when he interrupted and asked, "Actually Vaani, what do you feel about relationships?" "Sorry, what? As in what kind of relationships?" I asked. "How our generation boys and girls are," he said, "have you ever observed how they get into a love relationship? They try to impress each other by agreeing on each other's likes and dislikes, by being someone they actually aren't, it's something like opening a soda bottle," he explained "the moment the fizz goes, all that you are left with is nothing! That's how it has become nowadays; two people start talking to each other, they are all excited and enthusiastic about each other and what next! As soon as the excitement is over you face each other's reality and end in break-ups which is the sad phase. They do no good to each other by being like this, it just increases the complications that they have to eventually face, that's all." "Hmm..." was all I had to say when Sahil was actually letting my fizz out in his own ways. "See, Vaani," he continued again, "Since the time we met each other, which was just last month, you have been messaging me and that's really nice of you to be so friendly. But then somehow I can see that you are getting inclined towards me and have that excitement to hurry up things and get into some love affair kind of a thing." "Oh God, this guy is too direct, where do I run?" is what I was thinking while he was blabbering. Or at least, I felt like he was blabbering. I couldn't think straight because of all the nervousness! "Vaani, what I personally feel is that people should be purely friends first, they should know each other completely, and beyond that, if they are compatible things automatically move on to the next level, and it's then that they move for good. Because in such a case there is no soda bottle and fizz concept that intervenes, and then they can be best friends in a relationship for a lifetime." "Hmm..." is what came out from me again. I mean what else could I have said to all this lecturing? Forget the fizz; I was feeling like plain and still water. Ok, I agree that it was honest and it was nice of him but he literally took all my fizz and excitement away.

CHAPTER 4

"Take this number, he is the uncle who is in contact with the dental school's principal, he will arrange a meeting for you," said my mother. She had visited our new house in the medical college campus for the first time, but more than being excited about that she was worried about my well-being and my job. Well, any parent would have been the same I think. I was all happy in Hyderabad, earning decent money to support myself, and even planning a trip or two every now and then, in a respectable position and in a good work culture. Above all, I loved the southern part of India. Leaving everything and coming back had made me a little dull, and then who could have figured that better than my own parents. "But I don't want to approach him through someone mom," was my immediate reaction to that. "*Arre beta* approaching someone for a job works differently here, and then there is no harm in meeting him through a common contact. It just makes things easier," she explained. "But what if he gives me any stupid position to work as, what if I don't like it, I can't even say no because I have to oblige him. I don't want to get stuck mom. Why don't you understand?" I argued. AHH! Somehow I always got argumentative with my mother for anything and everything; it will be rare for me to remember as to when I had spoken to her peacefully last. There were two reasons for this; one both of us always had our own point of view for everything and second she was always in a hurry and gave an expression as if something was going on in her mind all the time. That had never ever allowed me to open up completely with her. But somewhere I knew that she was right. The work culture, especially in my field was way too different in Lucknow. More than work, the culture was all about hierarchy, need for contacts, and internal politics. Not only was it difficult to get a job there, but also it was difficult to maintain it.

Later that evening I called Manav, academically he had been my junior in the dental school but he was a very good friend of mine. “Manav yaar, I don’t want to be stuck here. Somehow I don’t even want to get a job here, what is the use of working for the peanuts they pay, and forget that, there is just no work satisfaction. Look at what all procedures we did back in college. And here? There is hardly anything to do!” Manav knew all the do’s and don’ts about me, he handled me completely well in any situation. “Relax Vaani. You always have the say. Put across very clearly as to what you are expecting from the job. Give it some time and at the end of the day the choice is all yours.” But whatever anyone said I knew what was going on in my mind all the time. Nevertheless, Manav was always comforting to me.

Me and Manav had been friends for some good three years then. I remember how he was when he had joined for his post-graduation, all in shivers before his first presentation. I had sat down with him for one entire evening on the day prior to his presentation and boosted his confidence. He was too curious about everything. I hadn't really seen a student like that till I met him. But on the contrary, he was never too confident about himself all because he never scored well. I pity the Indian grading system sometimes, or in fact, most of the times, because how much you know or how much you want to know never matters. All that matters are some scores and some medals. I wonder if any of the gold medal holders, I being one myself, knew as much as this guy. "Vaani," Manav explained, "you have set up your house there, to move away from Sahil and work somewhere else is always an option, but then don't you think you will be more stable there and at the end of the day no matter where you go you have to get back to where your husband is."

With all the forced efforts from people around me I felt like everyone was trying to hold me back in Lucknow. They said things will improve with time, they said I will get adjusted and adapted to live in the city and to live with Sahil. I am not too sure if everyone felt the same after their wedding but for me, it was as if I was being somewhere I never wanted to be, as if something somewhere was missing.

CHAPTER 5

It was almost one year after the day when Sahil lectured me on his soda bottle and fizz concept that he started calling me almost regularly. Both of us were in the final year of our graduation then; those regular calls started when we discovered that we had some things in common to discuss, which was either our subjects or some serious things in the society, or at times about how we would want our things to be in future. It was during these discussions that he found my interest in research, teaching, and academics and he motivated and guided me to prepare for my post-graduate entrance exams. There were times when I was upset and needed to let my things out, and there were times when I was happy and wanted someone to just listen to me. Be it anything, Sahil had become my best buddy to share everything. That phase of excitement and the need to impress however no longer existed; no wonder he had done a great job in letting my fizz for him out of me. For me, he was my perfect "phone-a-friend."

Interestingly the picture on the other end had started changing a little. Sahil was showing all the signs and symptoms of getting inclined towards me those days. He used to recharge with a small top-up every day just to call me and he was more and more interested in knowing what was going on in my personal life. “So how do you feel will be the guy whom you will want to get married to Vaani?” He asked me one day, this came to me as another bouncer and I hoped that he wasn’t in a mood to start with a lecture again after I told him about my choice of guy, similar to what he lectured after he asked me what I felt about relationships a year back. “Hmm… my kind of guy,” I said, I remember I used to have all assorted qualities one from each end of the pole to frame the list of qualities that I expected in my kind of guy. “He should be the bad guy kinds,” I continued, “someone who is good-hearted but then with a bad temper so that I can calm him down every now and then, who is self-made and is not dependent on what the previous generations passed on to him, who can be a good listener but doesn’t bore me either.” “And how about looks?” Sahil interrupted, “as in do you feel that he should be too tall or with a gym built and all?” “I never gave it a thought actually, I believe looks are never constant so that’s something I never relied on, and then as far as height and weight are concerned, obviously, I will not sit and record every guy’s body mass index and then select my guy.” I laughed.

I had met Sahil just once till then, it was with my girl gang almost more than a year back. We had met in a restaurant where we all sat and then Sahil and his friends had left early. Maybe if I would have met him more often I might have noticed that he was a lean and short guy and he just wanted to be sure whether I was ok with my guy being lean and short.

CHAPTER 6

"No I think I will look too thin in this," I said "and look at this one, I feel this isn't as smart. Oh God help me what do I wear!" I sat in despair and looked at Vilosha. "He is your cousin lady, what would he like to see me in; Indian or Western clothes, dressy or simple clothes, guide me please." Sahil was finally coming to meet me from Agra where he was pursuing his graduation then, and me being me was on cloud nine again. "Dress up in a nice *salwar kameez* Vaani, it suits you best. And then by the way *bhai sahib* is a very simple guy so for him it doesn't really matter what you wear. Dress up according to my likes and dislikes, after all, I will be your sister-in-law madam," she laughed. Vilosha was one of those characters, who loved teasing others. "Blaa! Alright lady," I said and left. This was going to be my second meeting with Sahil. The first one was unplanned and we had met like strangers, but now that we knew each other very well because of the long conversations that we had every day over the phone, I was conscious about my looks and clothes. Following Vilosha's advice, I decided to dress up in a nice sleeveless *salwar kameez,* which was Indian and was a little trendy, I looked smart but decent enough for my second official meeting with Sahil. Later that evening Vilosha along with some other friends of mine waxed my arms to prepare me for my sleeveless outfit and decided on my little accessories to match with it. I was thrilled. I don't remember if I slept properly that night.

I wouldn't call it a date with him though, because Vilosha the possessive sister decided to accompany me the next day. We hired an auto and headed towards the mall where we had planned our meeting. On our way she continuously narrated about how things were in her family, how Sahil was during his childhood days etc. Little was she aware that Sahil and I were better friends than what she thought we were and I already knew the stories that she was narrating to me then. But I didn't want to dishearten her and so I listened to everything that she told me like a new story. As we reached the mall we found that Sahil was already waiting for us at the entrance. In his blood red t-shirt and casual blue jeans, he looked different than what I had imagined him to be like. He was munching something and gave us a friendly hello from a distance. Unlike the last time when we had met for a few minutes and barely knew or interacted with each other this time I knew who this guy was, what his ambitions were like, and what his likes and dislikes were. It was just that I was seeing what my phone-a-friend looks likes in person. I noticed how he talks, what his expressions were like when he says something, how he interacts with others and what was it like to spend time with him. It's very different to know a person over a technological mode of communication and in direct communication. And then it's so different the way we are with them in either of those two situations. Even though Sahil and I knew each other well and had shared many of our secrets and plans in our interaction over the phone, that day in front of me he looked like a completely different man and even I behaved like a stranger. "Your voice sounds so different," I laughed. "Oh yeah both of you have never met each other properly right," said Vilosha assessing the entire situation. "Ya, but we know each other very well by now and that is why I thought I will plan coming here so that I can see both, my sister and my friend," he said. While he and Vilosha spoke about certain family matters, I continued to notice him. He was short, not too lean not too fat, and fair, more than fair actually he looked bright. It wouldn't be wrong if I say he had some glow from within. Maybe when you are full of positivity it shows. We spent most of our time eating, drinking, and chit-chatting about our respective colleges, about how we deal with patients, about how things were in our family and so on and so forth.

Later that evening, Sahil had to take a bus back to his city and Vilosha had some work pending in the hostel so she decided to leave early. I accompanied Sahil to the bus stop, and we got a good half an hour time alone in the auto that we took when we traveled to the bus station.

"It was nice to see you, Vaani," he said, "Hmm ya, same here" I smiled at him. But to my surprise I was in tremors from within. I barely spoke for the entire half an hour. In fact, I was too conscious to even look at him. For the entire duration that we traveled I was trying to avoid any contact with him. The auto driver kept looking at us in the rearview mirror every now and then but he had no idea that we were two timid and shy people who were still getting to know each other and he had no chance to witness any teenage romance between us. I thanked God when the bus station came, rushed out of the auto to get some air, looked away and said, "Ok ya, safe journey. Bye!" "Wait," Sahil said, "look at this girl! You blabber anything and everything over the phone and you aren't even looking at me straight now." "No no, I am fine. I mean we speak so much over the phone, so there is not much to speak I guess." I explained. "I see," he raised his eyebrows, "anyway, my bus will leave in another ten minutes, so I will push off. And by the way, there is a little thing that I bought for you." He took out a small gift-wrapped box and gave it to me. "And please don't be in a hurry to see it. Get back to your hostel, freshen up and then open it. And after that... do call me; I will be waiting to talk to you."

CHAPTER 7

"Who has the patience to change clothes and get fresh!" I said to myself, threw the bag that I was carrying away, and opened the box that Sahil gave me as soon as I reached my hostel room. Inside I found a red colored photo frame with little hearts that formed its border and a small little teddy bear that sat at the edge of it which appeared to be holding the frame. More than the frame, what he actually wanted to give me was the little love note which he had put in the empty space which the frame had for putting pictures. I don't remember how many times I read the note that day and in the days that followed. It read as follows,

"I don't know what is there in you that pulls me towards you, your intelligence, your behavior, your innocence or is it just the way you talk, just the way you are. If at all I am in any confusion, tension or trouble then the only thing that I need to get out of any of this is just a little thought about you. If I am not mad then certainly I am in love with you!"

Contrary to my normal reaction of reaching cloud nine on any exciting thing that ever happened to me, after reading this which would have been too exciting for any other girl I was rather blank! There was a sudden surge of mixed thoughts that occupied my mind. I knew Sahil was showing interest in me but somehow maybe I wasn't waiting for a proposal from his side. Maybe I had a feeling that I lost a very good friend, you see how love relationships are, you barely remain as friends with each other. Or maybe I wasn't in a state of mind to think about Sahil in a whole love way. After all, my fizz had been taken out long back! To be honest I also do not know what I actually had in my mind at that particular moment when I read this. It's not for no reason I guess that there are so many jokes on understanding women. Trust me, every woman feels that she is complicated at some point in her life. And for me, this was just one such moment.

I went out in the corridor with my earphones plugged in to look around so that I could allay my thoughts a little. "Vaani," someone screamed my name. I looked behind, there were three colleagues of mine with their coffee mugs in hand who were possibly gossiping over some matter in the hostel over coffee. "Babes you back! How was your meeting, we heard you met Vilosha's cousin today!" AHH! So I am the talk of the gossip. Fire in the jungle! I thought. Any little news in the hostel is actually like fire in the jungle; even if it's a spark it becomes big within no time and spreads all over. "It was a casual meeting," I said. "Well tell us more about how he is," the girls seemed curious. I didn't pay a lot of attention to their curiosity. I just laughed a little, cracked a joke or two about the meeting, plugged my earphones again and got back to my room with my own heavy thoughts.

I was never a casual person and did not want people to have false hopes for me. That is probably why I was thinking so much about Sahil's note. According to me, people needed to be too strong emotionally to have casual flings. Oh yes, I did have the fizz in the soda and got on cloud nine for little things but I guess I knew how to control my fizz and where to step in for more. Maybe even I was someone who was as cautious as Sahil before stepping into something which could be more serious. It was a little ironic that I was thinking so much before calling the guy who was giving me thrills and blushes just a couple of hours ago after he had actually proposed to me.

CHAPTER 8

"Yawn!" Yet another yawn since the morning, I wondered what to do; sitting alone at home for the entire day is a real pain, especially when you are a little quicker at your household work. Television was never a good time pass for me either; I rather believe it blocks your brain. Idiot box! That's what my mother used to tell me it was when I was a kid. But yes anyways our new house finally had a television with almost all the channels in Hindi, English and regional languages playing. I had subscribed to the regional channels as well just to make sure that I kept revising my Kannada and Telugu which I had learnt during my stay in the South and I was so proud of. Sahil and I had decided to get one big thing in the house at a time, so any big expenditures like television, air conditioner, and some major furniture were split as one every month and then of course in all this we had to accommodate a car as well. Sahil was planning everything from his expenses because I did not have any job and then he did not want me to spend my savings till I started earning again.

We made one of our rooms as our master bedroom where we had accommodated Sahil's study desk and books as well, whereas the other room had the television and we had kept it for relaxing or for "me" time. Sahil and I used to take turns to spend our time in the other room, at times he sat with a book or two to read something there and at times I was there watching TV, chopping vegetables or painting something. It made an ideal place to relax because right outside the window of the room there was a big Ashoka tree with pretty little birds that always chirped and made us happy. On purpose I had kept my almirah with my belongings in the second room making Sahil feel privileged to get the master bedroom closet all to himself. During the daytime, I used to sit doing most of my work there.

On one such day while I sat writing my to-do-works list, my mother's message popped, "What about the locker, did you go to the bank??" God! These private banks or even the government banks for that sake never have the availability of locker immediately. Just after the wedding, Sahil and I had opened a joint account for the sole purpose of getting a locker and here I was four months down and still no luck. I called them up immediately to ask when I could come down on an urgent basis, "We are sorry for the inconvenience madam, but this is the main branch and thus the locker allotments take a little more time," said the so-called personal banker over the phone. "You guys are a private bank," I argued "and my only purpose to open an account with you was for convenience and to my surprise, you are making me run for every little thing every fortnight. I want a locker by this week no matter what!" I said. "Sorry ma'am, let me check," he said, "Wednesday, 18th is it fine ma'am?" He asked. "Ya fine. I will be there and make sure you don't send me off with some stories this time, I have to travel a good twenty kilometers to reach the bank," I said and hung up. Eighteenth June, I marked on my to-do-list, eighteenth June! I recalled it was the same date when I had finally and indirectly accepted Sahil's proposal, almost three months after the day he had given me that note.

"See Sahil, you should understand I don't want that simple a life. I mean, we aim to do good for the needy people in future which is primary and we will do it. But then I don't want anything at the cost of my own living. I want a good house and all good basic facilities myself, that is important for me. I am being honest, I am a little materialistic as well" I said after I finally told him that even I felt he was good and I liked him. I was never direct in saying the so-called three magical words. Women! I told you they are a little complex! "Yes, Vaani, even I will never let your personal requirements suffer, and then even I want a good house and good amenities, who says I will make you stay in shacks." He said, "we will do everything slowly, we will work hard, help people and help ourselves too, you don't have to worry." he continued. "But how can you like me, I mean I don't even think I am that good looking." I argued again. Basically, I was never too confident about my looks, at times I thought I was too lean, at times I thought my complexion wasn't as uniform, and at times I thought my nose was not as sharp. "I never go by looks, Vaani," he said, "See, it means I don't look good and still you like me, isn't it. Man! Please don't compromise and you better go for someone else," I was upset. "Who says you don't look good, you are super cute and by the way your eyes are beautiful and your smile is very attractive." Now you are talking I said to myself and laughed internally. "Ok then sleep time," I said and we hung up. Similar to me, Sahil did not give any cloud nine reactions when I showed positive signs for his proposal. On the contrary, he sounded very casual about it. But the moment I hung up the call his message popped. It was a forwarded one and had many smiley emoticons after which it read as *"I am sending you hundred smileys, keep them under your pillow, it's one for each day for the next hundred days so that you can be happy each day when you wake up."* Immediately after that message, yet another message popped up which was his again but was not a part of the forwarded message; it said, "Ok actually don't keep those smileys under the pillow, I will stay by your side and make you smile for your entire life." Yes, I was sure that Sahil was in love with me and he did want me to stay by his side forever. And me? Well! I was just going with the flow.

CHAPTER 9

Sahil used to visit Lucknow to meet me more often now, his often was once in five months. Besides these visits, one interesting common spot that happened for us to meet was PULSE an All India medical fest organized by AIIMS, New Delhi. It invites students from all medical/dental institutes across the country and even the Delhi university colleges participate. PULSE is highly eventful. It's flooded with people, all young doctors can be seen in extra-curricular action here, some in the literary events, some in cultural and some in sports. Events wind up by seven or so in the evening and it's then that some fun follows, some celebrity visits, some music bands perform, or some stand-up comedy artists make us laugh. I was in two thoughts to visit PULSE that year. But when Sahil called and told me that he and some of his friends will also be visiting, I immediately got my bookings done. Basically, his Lucknow trips were only for a couple of hours and then since it was my hometown I was never too comfortable to meet him because of the many known faces that I had in town. Delhi would be fun I thought, specifically in a fest where you don't need to hide from your uncles and aunties seeing you.

Moreover, it was for one entire week that we would have stayed in the same city. I packed the best of my outfits and accessories, got my hair blow dried so that I look more groomed up and attractive and not to forget carried my aviators along. During the day, Sahil was occupied with some or the other sports event, table tennis, cricket, football, badminton... he participated in all of them...and me! I just used to wait for him to get free after my literary events were over. I was more into the debate and elocution which occupied me for a maximum of one hour.

One evening we both got free early and decided to spend the rest of the day together. We sat in one of the college canteens and ordered some noodles and coffee. "My family doesn't understand the present generation at all," Sahil said, "they are completely against love marriages, forget caste and culture," he continued. "But then how do you think that things are going to work out in future?" I asked, "See Vaani, things will take some time. As of now we are still a few years away from wedding, but yes, even after I initiate I will take a good amount of time to make my parents understand things and to get them acclimatized about the whole love marriage thing. I don't want to hurt them and take any step and then I want you as my life partner; I am sure about both the things" he explained. "Waiting is fine Sahil, see anyway my parents are all cool! For them, the guy should be good and in a working condition, that's all." I laughed. "So you can be sure that neither I nor my family will be of any trouble to you. You can take all your sweet time and figure out things at your end," I assured him. "That's really nice of you, but then you have to understand that both our families have very different traditions, yes they will care a lot about you once things settle down," he said. "*Arre baba,* why are you so worried? Be assured that your family is my family and then I know that there are some variations in the culture we follow. But then obviously you will stay with me to guide me and help me adapt to the culture isn't it? So just chill because in case we get married then you will have the best or rather the best-est wife ever!" I laughed again. He held my hand, smiled and said, "You are always so supportive, thanks for everything." I smiled back and said, "Just noodles? I thought you were ordering *samosas* as well," we laughed. I always had the habit to interrupt a serious discussion with a light talk, but Sahil continued, "I will take you to my village. We have a huge plot of land there. We will open a hospital for the people of that region. So many kids suffer from Japanese encephalitis in my native area, both because of unawareness and because there are no good facilities nearby. I want to master in Pediatrics and go there, I want to make some change for my people," he looked thoughtful. "And then we can set up your dental clinic in the city which is just half an hour from there so that you are not deprived of the basic things in the village, stay in the city and keep visiting to manage both your clinic and our hospital," he continued. I looked around at some other students in the canteen who sat there laughing and teasing each other. All of them looked in a fest mode, and here we were, discussing plans for almost after ten years from then.

While Sahil continued to speak to me I got lost in my own thoughts, thinking how strange it was how so many young people of my age around me were involved in casual flings and how this guy had all the dedication for me. Now or later, here or far I was always a part of his plans. I must have done some good deeds to have a partner who was still my friend first, with whom I could discuss or share my best and worst without any worries, with whom I could be myself without even a second thought, and who I was sure would love me with all his heart despite anything that happened. "What are you thinking about so deeply? Are you listening to me? I was saying we will work hard and do our best," he interrupted. "I am and I will always be there with you Sahil, in your best and in your worst, we will work hard and get through all big things slowly. I feel those who are blessed to inherit everything rather miss out on the smaller pleasures in life, the pleasure which one has when one works hard and get things for oneself. Our first television, our first car, our own house! There is a time for everything, and slowly we will have our time too. We will make our empire!" I said that staring into the empty space in front of me and as soon as I turned towards Sahil, I found him looking at me deeply. He drew me near him, held my hand and gave me a peck on my cheek. I was quiet and I felt his hand sliding down towards my waist. I held it, pushed him aside and said, "There is a time for everything, wait till we are together for good!"

Sahil and I stayed with each other as firm pillars of support throughout the time while we were studying and becoming doctors. After our graduation, we had to appear for a difficult All India exam in order to pursue our post-graduation. Though he was a medical and I was a dental graduate we did have some common subjects between us and we studied them together. Almost every day during the time of evening snacks, we spoke for some time and discussed some points, asked each other questions etc. Of course, we were still in different cities but stayed connected through our mobile phones. At that time there was no Whatsapp, video call or unlimited conversations over the internet data. There were just the mini recharges through cards and limited conversations, our time was set and we didn't waste any extra penny over prolonged conversations because we were still students. While Sahil qualified and bagged himself a seat to pursue Pediatrics, I couldn't get any seat in the first attempt. I remember I was broken, I had given up. I tried writing some exams to go out of India as well but nothing fell in place for me. Sahil had joined a new college, he was again in a government setup based in a different portion of North India and was busier than before, unlike the time when we both used to discuss and talk now it was me all alone. Despite the work schedule

Sahil took as much time as he could to keep me going. He pushed me to prepare for the entrance again, he showed me the bright side of things and kept me motivated. My strict schedule and discipline for that entire one year finally got me through the examination in the following year. I joined to specialize in the kids' teeth!

My fortune took me to the southern portion of India. I always had a fascination about the south, in fact, I loved the south Indian cuisine equally well. As a rule, whenever I went to eat out I ordered the same conventional *Masala dosa.* People said that's because maybe I had a connection that side. But me and Sahil didn't lose our connection. For the three years that I stayed in Karnataka for my post-graduation, I held to both Sahil and to my schedule the same way. I worked very hard to acquire good skills and to learn more, I was completely engrossed in my subject like a dedicated scholar. I didn't want any medals or laurels, I just wanted to learn more so that I could do my best in future. I traveled back home less often, my friends were my support. I learned the local language and made the place as my own. I never felt like an outsider, no one made me feel like one either. It was after a year of my stay in the college that I was introduced to Manav. We bonded in the library and over the textbooks and we had no idea that we were bonding to stay with each other for a really long time, we were bonding to experience the purest form of human relation which was friendship.

CHAPTER 10

"Your resume is surely very impressive, Vaani," said the head of one of the Dental Institutes in Lucknow, "But how about clinics? There are a few people I know and to whom I can mention about you. They don't pay as much and may not give you a lot of work, but then you will be occupied," he continued. For what is my resume impressive then? I thought. I had invested almost nine crucial years of my life in my dental education after school, I worked my best, had a handful of gold medals and then he said I won't get as much work. All that he could get me was something to keep myself occupied! Wow! Thanks, Mr. Principal! I thought in my head, but then I can cook, I can write something and I can do some other creative work to keep myself occupied in that case.

I was in the city for eleven good months already but was still without a routine job. Dentistry in India or in fact in the north of India I believe was far from reaching its actual potential. There were more graduates but much lesser opportunities, more demand but no awareness. Somehow the healthy competition, innovation, and zeal to do the best which I had seen in Hyderabad, had taken me to a whole different thought process. I couldn't think of just some work to keep myself occupied without deriving any work satisfaction. With the best of resume and qualification and with the zeal to teach and guide I was still at home.

Till the time I got married, I used to laugh on the entire women empowerment thing but all of a sudden I could feel that it wasn't really easy to be a woman most of the times. You can't decide where you want to settle because that call has to be your husband's, you can't get stable in a fixed agency for work because you don't get to decide where you settle, you take a break to get pregnant, raise your child and if needed quit your job for the same. Of course, these are beautiful and different phases of life but then women, or rather most of the women are never acknowledged in the right way for all the compromises they make.

Lately, something which I was facing when I visited outside of the medical college campus was eve-teasing. Most of the men on my way scanned me from top to bottom, passed teasing remarks and tried to accidentally touch me here and there. Yes, I was careful on my way, but then why did I have to be careful? Why couldn't I be just me? There were so many things that I faced every day and there was nothing that I was able to do about it. "I will go and work in Delhi till I get something here," "I had told Sahil's mother one day." "Delhi! Why? Sahil is here, you have to take care of him, things don't work like this after wedding!" Was the immediate response that I had got from her. "But he is not there for the entire day, his day starts at seven thirty in the morning and he is not back until eight in the night. Even after he is back he has to prepare for something or the other for the next day. Even the weekends are the same mummy no week off and no holidays, I go crazy sitting at home for the entire day like this." I had tried arguing. "You don't get everything in life, Vaani. Your family life is important and that should be your only focus now," she was firm. I don't know which family life was she talking about, I used to have almost all my meals alone, I used to do all the travel, all my work alone, and then I wasn't asking for anything too big. I had told her that I will be back as soon as I will have some provision in the city. By sitting idle like this I didn't want to lose all my skills, I didn't want my mind to be a devils workshop. Once I was sharing my state of mind with one of my ex-colleagues and to my surprise, she said, "Use this phase to plan a child. That is also one work, finish it off!" Wow, I didn't know that! Is what I thought in my head that time. Why can't the two people decide when and how they want to plan a family, why can't the women be mentally prepared and stable by their career to step into that big decision? Why the expectation from her to quit everything, including her likes, dislikes, and her true nature, to bring up the family while the men progress, accomplish and succeed. What is the whole use of the processions about educating the girl child I thought, when at the end of the day nobody cared about whether she was able to even put that education to use or not, when she was still considered secondary when it came to working, and when her priorities were still set by people around her.

Anyways, I had kept myself busy in some of my hobbies and was trying to follow a routine despite everything that was going on around me. One evening we went out to attend a party which some company had hosted for Sahil's department. They treat you like kings and queens no doubt; we were received warmly and were immediately served with the best of starters and drinks. Everyone was dressed up formally and it was more like an official meet with a small presentation by the company followed by dinner and light talks. We heard about some new products that they were launching, why their medicines were better and so on and so forth. After that small meeting was over we had an awesome drive within the college campus, five of us in one friend's car. It was beautiful! We rolled down the windows and let the breeze touch all of us; while we drove we were surrounded by the greens on the sides and an empty road in front. In fact, to my surprise, there was a lake on the campus with some deer around it. Nature is truly the most mesmerizing thing, something that you can never have enough of. With some nice music in the car and a drive like this I was in some world of mine own for a while. I forgot my entire struggle, I forgot all that people said to me when I approached them for jobs. I felt at ease, I was relaxed. After I was back home I realized that I was too tired. My day had begun at six in the morning with some household work, then running around to meet people with my resume, and then cooking followed by the party. I looked at the watch and it was past midnight already. I went to the kitchen to wind up some work when Sahil came and held me from behind; this was an indication that he wanted to have a good time. "Yes, Mr. Husband?" I yawned. "Do all this tomorrow," he said and took me inside the bedroom. He came ahead to kiss me, I tried to resist a little but then the usual followed.

There was an emptiness that I always had inside of me. It was there during the day when I was all alone doing nothing, it was there while I was traveling or talking to someone, and it was still there when Sahil was with me or over me. That day while Sahil embraced me and while he tried to show me the best of his affection, I was still blank and stared at the rooftop. All of a sudden my past flashed in front of me. I looked away and tried to run from those thoughts but the more I tried distracting myself the more they forced themselves into me. I had never let anything of the past cross my mind ever since I had left Hyderabad because I wanted to give my best to Sahil. I wanted to give everything a fresh start. But perhaps all the negativity that I was facing then, took away all my strength to stay strong and in that one moment I could suddenly feel the same winds which I had felt that day on the rooftop restaurant in Hyderabad. In that one moment my mind finally stopped struggling to fight against the thoughts that wanted to enter inside of it ever since I got married. In that one moment when I completely gave up on fighting with my thoughts, all that came to my mind was Akash.

CHAPTER 11

I had lived one life with him; laughed with him, cried with him, travelled with him, worked with him, listened to the music with him, spent time at his home, bonded with his parents, watched movies with him, sat in the silence with him, woken up with him...slept with him! I don't know how and why I accidentally browsed this website of some dental hospital in Hyderabad. I don't know how and why I even thought of applying for a job in that place almost two thousand kilometers away from my home, where I had never been and where I did not have anyone. Perhaps it was to find another way of living, perhaps it was to know a different culture, perhaps it was to make a home away from home, or perhaps it was just to find Akash.

It was almost three months after I had finished my post-graduation and my wedding was far from happening; because as Sahil had warned me before itself his family was taking a lot of time to agree for our wedding. My parents had visited their house once where we got an indirect no from Sahil's father, but despite that Sahil wasn't ready to give up on me, "There is no reason to say no Vaani!" He always said, "we are from the same state, and for society's sake from the same caste, yes we do differ marginally in our traditions because of the regions that we belong to but that's, of course, no reason to disagree. Give it some time; I have been talking to my dad consistently about it. I don't want them to feel bad either. Things happen with efforts and persistence. We will surely make it." "Yes, of course, I am all cool take your time," is what I said in response. Both of us were from the state of Uttar Pradesh, he being from the eastern portion and me being from the central portion. But within a span of the few kilometers that separated our families lay a lot of differences, a lot of circus in my words. Because of the slight change in language, and some differences in the beliefs, two very similar human beings were discouraged from getting married. The Gods must be laughing somewhere, I thought! Anyways I wanted to use this no-study, no-wedding phase to explore my work a little more, unable to find any work in my own city I randomly landed up in Hyderabad.

"But Vaani, you are in a different city, rather in a different state than where we are! Are you planning to relocate?" Asked the head of the recruitment section from that dental hospital in Hyderabad when she called me after probably looking at my resume. "Yes, ma'am that is the reason why I sent my resume to you," I said casually, while I was half lying down and was actually browsing my Facebook and thinking, 'who is going to go there for work man!' "Ok then Vaani what you can do is come down for an interview first," said the lady over the phone, "you can see how our setup is, how we work, and we can simultaneously assess you; after which you can take your call and we can take ours," she continued. "Sure I will let you know about it ma'am," I said and hung up. The moment I hung up I had the entire plan in my head and I marked it in my diary as; *"Go to Hyderabad, visit these guys, see the setup and then obviously you aren't joining there so chill pill! From Hyderabad, visit Bangalore and Coorg!"* Basically, I just looked for opportunities to visit down south every now and then. After my college, I had been there for my convocation and then for my degree separately and now I had one more reason to visit another city. Below my plan, I added a note, *"Call Manav! Tell him to fix a plan with some more colleagues, Let the holidays begin!!!"*

I landed in the city of Nizams and found my way to one of my friend's place in the city! My friend wasn't there though, so all that I had to do was, be in her house with her parents for two days till my interview got over. "North chapati more, here rice more," said my friend's mother, who welcomed me very warmly to their house and was serving me rice and sambhar with some pickle and curd for dinner. "No chapati, you ok?" She asked. Basically, she was purely Telugu speaking and we were managing to converse in some sign language and tits and bits of English. "I am a rice lover aunty, and what you served me is something I love," I said and sat on the floor along with my friend's father. They insisted me to sit on the chair and table. But then I preferred sitting with the family on the floor in the hall, ate with my hand just like everyone else did and relished the sambhar, rice, and pickle like never before. It was a small two bedroom flat, which wasn't actually flooded with a lot of things. All that was there in the house were some basic furniture and basic electronics. No dazzling curtains or floor, no unnecessary home décor products either, and instead of the conventional room fresheners which people use nowadays the house had some sweet smell of natural jasmine flowers which were probably offered to God in the prayer room. I was overwhelmed by the simplicity of the house and also her parents. That is probably something that had always attracted me to the south of India more. "How do you plan to commute to Secunderabad, Vaani," asked her father. My interview was scheduled for the next day by the hospital at the other end of the city from where I was then. "Uncle, may be I will take an auto," I said. "Ok. But then you should be a little careful with these auto fellows, especially when you don't know the city and the routes so well, language though is not a problem in Hyderabad," he said, "everyone here can talk Hindi, though my wife may be an exception," he laughed. I laughed back and said, "Don't worry uncle, I will figure the route through Google maps and yes I will be careful for sure." We had little conversations about the weather, food, and people in Hyderabad, and how the city had changed a lot over the past few years with growing technology. He also told me about the upcoming developments and projects that were planned and how it would become even better in connectivity with the rest of the world in the years to come. Once we winded our dinner, I was all set to get a good sleep and all ready to appear for my first official job interview the next day.

I dressed my best to look like a professional for the interview in a neatly ironed white chicken *salwar kameez* and a small bindi on my forehead, I kept my hair half open and half clutched. Ready for the day, I went out where the city came alive to me! People seemed to be in the morning rush. Some were waiting at the bus station, while others were walking hurriedly towards the bus or the auto stop, the roads looked decent but the pedestrians pathway was dug down for some construction, the buses and autos drove through it and made the dust flow in the air. The morning sun was not as harsh, and there was a tinge of freshness in the air despite the dust around because it was November and I was assuming that the winter winds were showing its effects. As soon as I reached the auto stop I could hear the drivers shouting, "Charminar madam" "Hi-tech city madam," it was easy to find one to my destination and I headed through the busy roads of the city towards Secunderabad. Small restaurants and biryani corners were all over throughout the way. No wonder people said that it was the city which treats your taste buds the best with its spicy food. Besides these, there were a lot of medical and dental hospitals that I could see on my way as well. I was wondering the extent of competition that must be existing within the corporates. The traffic was quite a lot as in any other city, but yes the traffic police were active, aware and controlled it well. I had always been a keen observer of my surroundings but somehow I was noticing the things lesser than usual because I had the interview on my mind. I was frequently using my front camera to make sure that my bindi hadn't moved or my kajal hadn't smudged. Front cameras are one of the best invention's for girls I believe! More than just taking selfies, it acts as the best all-time pocket mirror that they carry. The long way that I travelled passed soon and finally, there it was, the yellow-red building that the lady had told me about over the phone. And there I was walking with my resume and other documents to face my first formal interview for a hospital which I had no intentions of joining!

"So have you done all the types of procedures that you have mentioned in the resume?" Asked Mr. Naidu, the chairman of the organization, who looked like a serious man. He had a dark complexion, was a little overweight and sat on the chairman's chair with a faint forced smile on his face, "Yes sir," is all that came out of me. "We are a private organization, we have some work ethics and there is a certain way in which we talk to and handle our patients. We do not expect the child specialist to get impatient with the children. More than your skills your ability to deal with them is important. Your credentials are good and you are trained in a very reputed college, but remember your attitude is the most important thing for us," he said. "I understand your concern sir and I will make sure if I am given an opportunity to work here I will put up the best of attitude and best of work." I was confident. "How about the CT scan machine, which one did you have in your college?" "I am not too sure about the company sir, but yes I know how it works and I can interpret CT scans sir," I answered. "How about your stability in the city, Vaani?" He asked next. "I mean, you are unmarried, and you belong to Lucknow, your parents aren't here either, can you promise us that you will stay here for two years?" Two years! I laughed in my head. Sir I am heading on a holiday, I wanted to say. Instead I said, "I don't want to give you any false assurances sir, all that I know at this point is that wedding is my priority and if it comes up I won't say a no to it. So I am here till maybe I am married and if by fate I get settled here then I may stay for longer than just two years," I smiled. "You can join from the next month, Vaani. And as a rule, you will be in scrutiny and probation period for one month. During this period we will assess your work and then take our final call," he said and handed my documents back to me. To my surprise I found myself canceling all my holiday plans in my head, and contrary to my idea of saying 'I will let you know' and then disappear to Coorg, I instead found myself saying, "Can I rather join tomorrow sir?"

CHAPTER 12

'Scared and conscious' is what describes my state of mind on the first day of my work. "Hello, I am Dr. Utkarsh, the clinic head for this branch. You have to keep meeting me on and off for the entire month for the work you do, the timings you follow etc.," said the man sitting in a small chamber with some documents spread all around him. Basically, as Dr. Naidu had notified me earlier, I was supposed to be kept under observation for the first one month of my work. This clause itself had made me say a yes for the job. My revised plan now was to work for one month and after which I thought I will tell them that it's too far from home and I can't really afford to be working in this city. I had done my calculations well, I could manage my Coorg trip, to and fro flights from Hyderabad, and even two new dresses in my probation salary. And I had been sitting idle for past three months so I thought I will work for some time and resign. Hmm, yes employees are crooked in their own ways you see.

Dr. Utkarsh's chamber was the first one after we entered the hospital from the reception area. More than a personal chamber, it was rather a space given for keeping all of the important hospital documents. From previous patient's records to basic stationery for the hospital, it had everything; and in between all these on a chair sat this fair and fit man with silver-rimmed spectacles. "Sure sir, I understand, every day while coming and going for this one month I will take care to report to you. I will follow up with you for all the treatments I do," I responded back politely and took his leave to look around. I was dazzled by the hospital setup. I did not know if all the corporates were the same. It was huge and I hadn't seen something that big exclusively for dentistry in my city at least. There were six separate chambers for the doctors to work in, and there was a separate room dedicated to cleaning and disinfecting the instruments. Each chamber was provided with its own laptop and internet connection, a small desk and chair for consulting and a CCTV camera fixed to record all that was going on in the clinics so that it could be monitored by the heads. Everyone around me was busy. Some were speaking to the patients, some were running around with patient records, some were in conversation with the nurses of the hospital, probably instructing them something. But irrespective of what they were doing, they also had one eye on me which if could speak would have said 'who's that? Some new doc! Or some patient!' Everyone was dressed up professionally and was wearing their aprons and nameplates. I was just looking around and wondering whom I should talk to when I spotted a short and quite lady who wore a neatly draped saree and stood in a corner in front of one clinic, staring at her smartphone. I went to her and introduced myself, "Hi, I am Shivani," She said. I noticed she had a uniformly round face with big eyes and prominent ears. She had tied her short hair into a neat ponytail and gave a timid appearance. "So, for how long have you been here, Shivani?" I asked her, "Four months," she said. "Wow, that's decent enough to know an organization. I guess you will be able to guide me about the place and the do's and don'ts etc." I winked, "Hmm ya slowly you will come to know. Where are you from by the way?" she asked me. "Lucknow," I said. "Lucknow! North! You came all the way from there to work here!" "Ya," I said "Yesterday was my first day in the city and today, here I am, at work with you." I laughed. Shivani smiled back but did not respond much to that. She was a quiet girl and seemed to be interested in her own business, perhaps which is why I found her available to talk to, unlike others. Honestly, I always had a feeling that most of the south Indian girls were like that, a little more to themselves, with no interest in unnecessary gossips or making thousands of friends, unlike in my side where everyone wanted to know everyone's whereabouts. But then I being a very talkative person myself, spoke to her about her graduation, college, hobbies, her native etc. Though she spoke less she didn't seem to mind talking to me and so I continued. I was relieved to find someone that I could speak to; because after all the bold efforts of joining a job on the very next day of my interview with no proper place to stay and no one to converse with after I went back to my friends place, in Shivani I found my first friend in the city!

CHAPTER 13

"Guess what, Manav!" I was all excited to speak to Manav about my work, so I used to call him as soon as I got any free time in the hospital. "These guys deal with patients so differently than we did in college," I continued, "It's like you cannot afford to make even one mistake! I am so scared, I don't know if I will be a good professional here. "Vaani," Manav responded, "you also don't know how good you are. I have all the faith in you. You will do a good job there. Don't get too conscious, it's just that in college you feel there is someone over you to guide you. But here it's more independent, so you are feeling different. You know it all. Go ahead, girl!" He motivated me. "But you should plan to visit me soon. It's a new place for me and your place is hardly two hours from here. Visit your home and meet me on your way." "Of course I will come soon," he said.

After one week of stay in my friend's house, I had managed to find a place for myself. Even though I did not plan to stay in the city for long, I didn't want to trouble her parents. I took a paying guest accommodation on rent; I had finalized it after a lot of visits in all nooks and corners of the city. All that I wanted was a neat single occupancy room, and to my good fortune, I had found something exactly similar to what I was looking for. "I want the rent two days before the first of every month Vaani, and be sure that you take care of your own things. We are not responsible for any loss, and yes also please take care that the extra lights and fans are always off, ok," said the owner of the accommodation, who was good but then way too professional. "Yes ok," I said and took the keys to my room from her. It was a small room with a single narrow bed where she had provided me with a mattress and a pillow. On one of the walls there was a big wooden construction where there were three small sections of cupboards, and two small extensions below it to keep books or other belongings. On the other wall there was a big window with a sliding mesh and glass attached to it so that the room was well ventilated, the window kept the room well-lit by natural light. There was a small wash-basin in one corner of the room which spoiled the show. But then I decided to ignore it. I had an attached bath with a water heater, and a television for myself as well. "Not bad, Vaani," I smiled after having a look all around. After my job, all that I needed was my own space in the city and I finally had it.

Once my basic routine in Hyderabad was set, I was free by my mind to explore the city and to connect with more people. "Let's go to Ramoji film city," I was all excited because Manav had finally come down to meet me on a Sunday. It's built on some crazy acres of land, with too much activity inside. We took a fancy looking red colored hop in hop out bus to take a tour through the film city eating and drinking on our way. We watched some live shows going on as to how a fight scene is shot and how the Indian epics are shot within the city. I was thrilled to see the way they had made so many sets inside, everything looked so real. The jail looked like we were actually in a jail, the beautiful gardens looked like we were actually somewhere abroad. In fact, there were also a few human figures that they had made and with the sounds that they produced for a moment, I thought they were real people! I was wondering about the extent of creativity that exists and I was surprised by what all people can actually do. After one round of our tour was over we sat amidst a children's park with some juices and chips for our chit-chat session. "What Is going on regarding your wedding, Vaani madam?" Manav asked. "Hmm...everything under slow progress," I was still looking around. "Sahil met his father just last week, he explained to him why he wants to marry me, he told him about my family background, about me." I said, "Great! Things should be at the edge of working out then," he was excited. "Not really," I continued. "This is the nth time that he has spoken to his father like this. He listens to everything quietly and at the end he just gives a blank response and talks about some other match for Sahil! Even his elder brother isn't taking any stand for us. I don't understand how the young crowd can behave like that? If the so-called young generation doesn't talk or isn't firm about things that should be changed then obviously such orthodox thoughts will continue to exist in our society. "Isn't that super weird man?" I smirked. "Hmm...right. Vaani, can I ask you something?" "Yes of course," I said. "Are you very sure that you want to marry Sahil?" He was blunt and straightforward, which of course he had all rights to be because he was very close to me and he knew me way too well. "See why I am asking you this is because it's not just the boy that you get married to; you have to be sure if you are ok with his family as well. Look at yourself, you are so independent, so outgoing, and so logical! Do you want to be stuck with all this? This attitude and behaviour that his family is carrying is not just for now. This will be your family, this will determine what your children learn." "But Sahil isn't like that. He is supporting me completely. He has been with me for almost six years now, he completely agrees that his family is unnecessarily complicating things and he is not someone who will choose to live with some false beliefs. Manav, he knows me, he listens to me and if he does no one else can impose their decisions on us in future as well." I explained. I always had this firm belief that Sahil and I have a very good understanding of each other and together we could solve anything that comes our way. "Vaani, you are talking too theoretically. I am sure he must be a really good guy and obviously that is why you have been with him. But think in all possible directions. It's not a mathematic equation that you are solving. Just because you two have been together for so long doesn't mean you go ahead regardless of whatever the circumstances are. Do you have that thrill for Sahil, do you feel woohoo! This is the guy I love and I should marry..." **Whistle** we heard the guards calling us from far which interrupted our conversation. The bus which we were supposed to take for our return to the main city was leaving and so we started walking back. Manav slept through the journey, and I just kept staring out of the window and thought about what Manav had asked me. No, I did not feel any thrill for Sahil. I never felt any, except for some fizz which I felt years back and which he had taken out! Since then yes he had been just a very close friend, and for the rest of the relationship that we had, I was just going with the flow.

CHAPTER 14

"We are shifting you to the new branch of the hospital Vaani. Are you sure you will be able to handle everything by yourself there?" asked the head of the recruitment department to me one day. The hospital had opened a new branch of theirs in the Hi-tech city area of Hyderabad and they wanted me to shift there. This was the place which had all the IT companies and which was an area flooded with many north Indians. "Hmm...yes, madam, I will handle it," I replied. "But how about your stability here in this city?" she asked. I did not have an answer to that question of hers which went like a bouncer ball over my head. Somehow I was liking the place, somehow I was getting connected to people and then things were just not working for me back in the north, I kept contacting some dental colleges there for a job but they always said a plain and blunt *No vacancy!* Back in my Lucknow city, there were no such dental corporate hospitals as well and so I had very limited work options. After thinking for a while I said, "Madam, for now, yes I am here until of course, some emergency comes at home." "Oh that is there for anyone," she smiled. "Ok so see we want you to head the branch, we want you to be the in charge of everything there right from the administration to your own work, and to others works as well. We have seen your work, you are good and so we feel that you will be able to take the charge well. If you have any doubts then you are always free to call any one of us and don't think you are all alone. We will keep visiting you often. I will sit with Dr. Naidu and decide about a team which will be working with you and under you," she said. What!!!! I thought in my head. It was something like what Dr. Utkarsh was where I was working now, I just joined I thought and such a big responsibility! Woo! So obviously I did not have the option to run anytime soon! "Welcome to Hyderabad Miss Vaani," I said to myself.

Wow, I don't have words for the new branch where these guys had sent me. It was all glamorous and good. We had a huge reception with coffee colored and cream sofas, posters all over with individual spotlights, a professional reception desk and even the corridors and the cabins looked very classy. I looked at myself and wondered how I was going to handle everything. The good news was that even Shivani was sent with me. Together, the both of us set up the basic things in that place, hired the junior employees, the receptionists and the assistants and got everything in order. In fact, within no time we started working as a team, it was a brilliant feeling to work together. I used to look for the smallest of occasions to host a mini-party in the hospital. Our mini-parties were comprised of some fancy samosas from one corner shop and something to drink. I also used to order the famous Hyderabadi biryani for the entire team whenever we finished any challenging case successfully. Such small get-togethers kept all of us motivated. Shivani and I had bonded extremely well and we didn't know how. She was some good ten years elder to me and stayed with her daughter and her husband. If something was wrong at her house, she used to discuss it with me. If I had any small or big requirement, I used to tell her about it with utmost comfort. We had found a level of understanding in each other, if I understood her family problems, then she was a patient listener to my adulthood issues. Simultaneously, we were completely engrossed in making our branch of the hospital the best. Once while I was listing out on what all diagnostic centers our patients needed, I figured out that we did not have any CT scan machine and neither did any nearby laboratory had it. "But Shivani ma'am, don't you think it's too cumbersome for people to travel twenty kilometers far and get just one investigation done. Nowadays everyone is so busy, and none of the people I contacted do the scan in their centers," I expressed my concern. I used to address her as madam because of her age and then I felt she deserved the respect. "Yes you are right. Why don't you contact Dr. Akash," she said, "he is the head of one of the branches of our organization. I have heard he refers his patients to somewhere nearby. You can ask him where he refers and we can do the same. He has been there for quite some time now so he will guide you for other things as well." "Oh is it, yes I should talk to him then. Thanks." I said. I did not have any clue as to who this Dr. Akash was so I asked my receptionist to dial in the branch where he was working. "Vaani madam wants to talk to Akash sir," said my receptionist as I waited and sat beside her, "Hello," I took over the phone. "Sir is having his lunch, madam," said the voice from the other end. "Oh ok, can you ask him to call me back?" "But why do you want to talk to him?" they asked again, "For your information, I head the hi-tech city branch of the hospital. Why would you ask me something like that? If there is anything that I want to be conveyed, I will do it myself," was my blunt response. "Oh sorry madam," they said and hung up. "What, why, when... why do they want to ask all this when they know a professional is calling!" I was angry. "No madam, maybe because he is a little famous that's why they would be thinking some girl is randomly calling to flirt with him," explained my receptionist. "Weird people," I was surprised, "as if I care!"

Sometime later while I was having my lunch, I got a call on my reception. It was Dr. Akash. "Yes you called me," said a strong manly voice from the other end the phone. "Yes sir. Sir I am Vaani. I heard you send your patients for CT scan in some center located around us. I just wanted to ask you the details of the center, so that we can also contact them for the same. I have tried my best but I am unable to locate any diagnostic center for CT scans nearby." "Hmm...so when did you join Vaani?" He asked and I told him everything about myself. "See I am a little busy with some patient right now. Give me your number and I will call you back and we will talk about it in detail later." All the branch heads had received a number with a common series from the hospital for internal communications and discussions. I gave him the last three digits of my official number. "No not the official one, give me your number where I can send you a Whatsapp message. If required I will forward you the details there," he said. "Yes sir sure," I said and gave him my number. But little did I know then about the turn that my life was about to take, and the storm that was just waiting to hit my life.

CHAPTER 15

"Hey Doc, its Akash this side," popped a message on my screen late in the evening when I was preparing for dinner. "Hello sir," I replied. "We don't send our patients for CT scans to any specific place around. If needed, they find a place and just get us the results." "Oh is it? Ok, thanks sir." I texted back. "So you seem to be a dynamic new branch head," he messaged again. I smiled at that and typed "No sir, not dynamic. I am still a learner. I have heard a lot about you though." I was typing fast. "Um hum! So I believe people talk about me. But then I don't really bother about the good or the bad they speak." He texted and soon after which there was another text that followed, "By the way, did you reach home or are you still working Miss sincere!" "No. Why would I? Of course, I reached home. I was just cooking something for dinner in fact." "Wow! So you gave your mom a break and you are cooking for her today is it?" "No sir, I stay in a paying guest accommodation. I don't belong to Hyderabad." I replied. "Aww...you stay alone, you must be bored after you are back,right? How do you pass your time?" "Hmm...it's been hardly any time since I am here actually. I am still getting acclimatized to the work and the place. So as of now, it's all cool." I texted back. "Oh yes! I forgot someone is the young and dynamic new head of the branch. From where will you get the time to think about anything else?" "*Saak Ayetu,*" I typed out of reflex! Basically it's a phrase in the Kannada language which means "enough." I being in Karnataka for my education had it at the tip of my tongue most of the times. "Hey how come you know Kannada!" Was the instant reply from Akash. "Oops I was about to say sorry for that, you understood? How come you know Kannada?" I asked. "Madam it's my mother tongue," he flaunted. "Oh is it? I am happy to know that I can talk in your language then," and after that I explained about my education, how I picked up that language, and how I could even sing songs in it. In the next one hour that followed after that, we texted and texted about our hobbies, native places, life in Hyderabad, our organization, food and what not. It was all so natural. I didn't even realize that we had been messaging for so long. I didn't put any efforts to text, and I didn't put any efforts to keep the conversation going. "Ok, let me have my dinner Akash sir before it's too late. I am too strict about my schedule mind you." I messaged him to end the conversation and to get going for dinner. "Oh yes sure, get going," he said and I finally rested my thumbs!

Later that night I received a call from Sahil, "How are things going?" he asked. Sahil used to call me almost every day to talk about my work and his work and about the progress if any on the wedding front.

Wedding talk was halted for quite some time now after his parents had told an informal "no" to my parents. I was not in a hurry to get married so it didn't really bother me that much at that point in time. "So far so good," I said. "The branch is picking up just fine and too much of work all the time," I continued. "Good, you are working hard," he was happy. "Ya I have to. There is a lot to learn. I spoke to one new senior colleague today named Akash. He seems to be a friendly nice guy. I texted him for quite some time. He is so much like me Sahil." I was all excited to tell him and so I vomited my entire conversation out to him. Basically anything good, bad or whatever it was, I had to tell Sahil. I don't know if I was used to it or because I knew he will understand but yes I did. He laughed and said, "So much like you is it? You just take no time to derive conclusions about people isn't it?" He laughed again. "What do you mean? You are mad ok. I can make out how people are and then I enjoyed texting him." I said. "Of course you should text him and talk to him if you like, I am just saying that you should not derive conclusions on who is how so soon," he explained. "You should go on a hill and meditate Sahil Baba," I made fun of him and laughed. "Soon, someday." He laughed too, and then the usual goodnights followed. I lied down to get some sleep but couldn't help smiling to myself. Till almost midnight I kept tossing and turning. "Young and dynamic branch head," I laughed and with a faint smile on my face I don't remember when I fell asleep.

CHAPTER 16

"Shivani madam, all your paperwork is pending, what's wrong with you?" I was loud. One afternoon while I was going through some files to keep in check with the administration that I handled, I found a lot of backlog and thus that reaction from me was obvious. "Ya I have to do it. No one from the reception reminds me and I keep forgetting it all the time," she said. "But I feel there is something really wrong with you nowadays madam. You look so dull." I was worried. "Nothing specific, I am just bothered about my daughter's health and so I keep forgetting I believe," she said. "Come on! Your daughter just had a little cough and cold. I know it's not that," I spoke like a confident friend who can't be fooled easily. "See you can share anything with me anytime," I assured her and got up for some work when she interrupted me and said, "Actually, you are right, It's about something else." I sat down again and quietly listened to what she had to say. "Vaani I changed my religion some one year back," she said and looked at me for almost half a minute. Maybe she was expecting me to give some shocking reaction, but ok is what I said. She looked a little comforted by that and went ahead, "It was due to some beliefs of mine and my husband's over our daughter's health. And our family is just not accepting things the way they are now." I was quite for a while and then I asked, "So was it so from the beginning or they have become against it all of a sudden?" "No they have always been against it. Now because of some ritual that has to be performed by us, these things have come to the fore again. They keep calling us all the time and are trying their best that things should revert. In fact, they say things like we aren't your parents anymore," she looked down at the floor and appeared quite heartbroken. Her daughter was seven years old and she must have been nearing some forty herself. Of course, she had the right to follow what she believed in and of course she had the maturity to take her own decisions. But then she had to face all this. Sometimes I laugh when I think how tied up we are in the social pressures around us for such little things. Shivani's parents were complicating things so much for her, and Sahil's parents were complicating things so much for him all because of something's which even they may not have justified themselves. All because of the big question, "What will people say?" I wonder who do we live for, ourselves or others. I think we decide a significant portion of our lives based on others opinions. The others can be anyone; may be from your own family and friend circle or people who don't even matter in your life.

"I don't know what you must be thinking about me," Shivani said interrupting the philosophy that was flowing in my mind then. “Madam, trust me I am the last person to think anything about you. It’s your decision and how does it really matter as to what your beliefs are as long as you don’t harm others, as long as you do your work sincerely? Take it lightly madam. Try explaining this to your parents. And if they still do not listen to you then perform whatever ritual they are saying for their happiness and keep following what you believe in. See, at the end of the day it’s all one and the same ok. It’s just that the forms we created of the same master are different. So chill and don’t find excuses to delay the paperwork,” I laughed. Shivani also laughed and she seemed to be much relieved because probably she finally found someone who did not judge her by the religion she followed or by the beliefs she had!

The serious conversation and thoughts were interrupted when my receptionist came and said there was a call for me on the landline number. “For me?” I was surprised and ran, “Hello, yes?” I answered. “Why don’t you answer your personal phone?” Asked a deep manly voice on the other end. “Sorry, who is this?” I asked. “Ahaan! So I have to remind the super enthusiastic branch head about me I suppose,” said the voice which I was beginning to recognize by now. “Oh! Akash sir!” I blushed and smiled to myself. “Ya it’s me! And by the way I hope you were not too busy,” he said. “No no I wasn’t working.” “I see. So did you sort out places for the CT yourself?” “No I did not sir. I thought I will rather follow what you told me. That should work fine." "Ya, that should be fine. Actually I had called to tell that there might be a patient that needs to be transferred to your branch. I will text you the details by the evening." "Sure sir." I said. "By the way, tell your receptionists not to give you random calls. I never told them who I am and they still called you. Tell them to be a little more careful," he sounded concerned. "Oh ok sir, sure." I was thankful. "And one very very important thing, be a little less formal Miss young and dynamic," he chuckled. I blushed again and then carefully controlled my expression as I found my receptionist starting at me. "Sure," I said and disconnected the call.

CHAPTER 17

Akash and I were regular on messages and calls since that call at the reception. Unlike previously when he was actually finding reasons to poke me, now it was without any purpose. He used to call me either while he drove back from work or at random. Once during our regular message session, he demanded a treat from me. I think that is the most direct way in which any guy says that he wants to meet you. Of course, we were colleagues but then our workplaces were different and so we had never met personally except in the common meetings where everyone minds their own business and leaves. "Treat, ya sure. Whenever you say," was my response to him because after all the conversations and little talks we had I also wanted to meet him. "I am free, free, free," he said. This enthusiastic way of talking was so typical of him. I smiled and messaged, "Wednesday, after the hospital hours then." "Done, but then there is a little condition, I will come and meet you only if you have a little vodka with me." Someday I had told him that I never had alcohol, and neither I wanted to try because I was rather high on life and so he wanted to make it a point that I should try it. I rather said a "No," to it to which he said, "Naa! Then we are not meeting. I don't hang out with traditional girls." "Is it?" I smirked. "But then sir, in that case, you wouldn't get a treat either," I argued. We stuck on our points but the date was still finalized. It was sometime in March end when the weather had just begun to turn a little hot during the day time but it was pleasant in the nights. Perhaps that was the reason why Akash chose a rooftop restaurant for us.

"Oh God why is my eyeliner getting here and there," I said to myself as I continued to dress up after rushing back from the hospital. He said he will reach directly from work but because my accommodation was right beside the hospital I rushed and changed into something more trendy rather than the monotonous everyday *salwar kameez*. A black and white sleeveless top with a black shrug on top of it and black jeans is what I chose to wear for the night. Under that I wore some three inches of heels. Wearing heels can be a little uncomfortable for many but then for tiny tots like me it's like, as if we walk over them. I rushed and reserved an auto for myself and while I was on my way, I got a call from Akash saying that even he was on his way. We were supposed to meet in a café within a mall. I was trying to keep my hair in position which was flying in all the directions in the open auto and of course Hyderabad winds were adding to the crime. I handed over some money to the auto fella as I got down and in fact I did not even bother to collect the change and ran towards the washroom to undo what the wind had done to my hair. While I was still having a final look at myself, he called again, "I am sitting here already. Come to the third floor." I took the escalators to go up and there I was on the third floor, and right in front of me was the NEWS café!

I felt butterflies in my stomach and tremors in my hands as I entered the place. Why I can't say, perhaps because we were meeting for the first time, perhaps because I thought I still did not know him enough to plan an outing with him, or perhaps because somewhere I was beginning to like him and I was not realizing it. I crossed the corridor to reach their rooftop segment and I saw him waving from somewhere far around a corner space. I smiled and waved back, after which the adrenaline took over, the tremors increased and I walked towards him. "So madam," he said and extended his hand. I shook hands with him did something with my hair again. I was getting a little conscious and sat down with a bewildered smile on my face. It was a pretty place and there was a young crowd around us. People were boozing, eating, laughing and enjoying the music that the café guys had played. We could see a portion of the hi-tech city area from where we sat; stylish and tall office buildings of the IT sector companies were well-lit, a small patch of well-maintained green which appeared to be some garden was seen far somewhere between the huge constructions and the roads were full of vehicles which were moving rather slowly. "Finally we meet," I smiled. He looked at me and then looked at himself and said, "It's good you can quickly change and come in your informal clothes. I rushed straight from the hospital and look at me, eww." "Yes true. I am freer in this but then it's alright. How does it matter, you work and you should be proud to be busy." I smiled again. "You are the philosophical best and I am the casual best," he said in his style. After that little chat the tension inside me disappeared, we got very comfortable with each other at once and ordered some common starters for both of us and some beer for him. Unlike how he was over the phone, he left the alcohol to my choice and I preferred not trying it and ordered some coke instead. As we chit chatted he took out a cigarette and lit it and then gave me a casual look and asked if I had any problems with smoke. To be honest, I have always had problems with smoke but then with him it seemed just correct and I said I had absolutely no problems. "As long as you know what you are doing, and as long as you know what your limits are it's alright; and then you are a grown up man and you know the good and the bad the helpful and the harmful." I looked at him and said that in my philosophical style. I don't know why again but whatever he did and said always seemed correct to me and I had nothing to argue. "Hold this" he said as he handed over that lit up cigarette to me, I took it and stared at it in excitement, while he took out his wallet and two of his passport size pictures from it, "This is how I looked back then in my college days," he handed over one to me. "And look at this other one which I got clicked recently, handsome no?" He said and flaunted. "Very," I laughed and gave them back to him. However, until he mentioned I hadn't really noticed him, with his chiselled jaw bone, long face, big and expressive eyes, he was certainly handsome. His hair looked thick with some shades of grey in between and he had an unshaven rough look which was certainly attractive. "I have had so many girls who used to like me you know. There is one very close friend of mine and now even her son talks to me," he continued to flaunt and I continued to smile at his girlfriend's stories. But then the usual me started about how weddings are, how affairs have become so casual nowadays etc. Woo, I thought I was behaving like lady Sahil and laughed in my head. It reminded me of the time when I was rather on the other side of the picture with a lot of fizz which Sahil had lectured out. After around two hours of our chit-chat session on the terrace restaurant he said, "Let's go and sit in the music section for a while." "After you," I said and we went to the section of the café where there was some cricket match playing on a big screen and the music was super loud for anyone to hear anything. I sat on a high table and he stood next to me with his beer. In a fraction of a second, he kept his hand over my shoulder, came near me and said, "I have two left feet, I just can't dance." "Oh is it?" I smiled, but I had a sudden sense of thrill that passed through me, I had never been so close to a guy before. After that he showed me two of his favorite dance moves and said that it was all that he could do and laughed. We shouted in each other's ears for the next five minutes and exchanged few one line conversations. Our little talks were interrupted by a call from his sister. It was past midnight already and he had to head back home. He drove me back till my accommodation on his bike. I enjoyed the ride and got down to say my final goodbye for the day. Even he got down and extended his arm. For a moment I did not know what that gesture was supposed to be. Such a philosophical illiterate that I was, and then somehow I figured that he probably wanted to hug me the way they do after parties when they part. In a sudden jerk I moved towards him and held his shoulder lightly trying my best to avoid any further contact. The tremors crept in again; I walked back to my accommodation and I was a little uncomfortable in my heels this time. I don't know where that discomfort came from; the heels where it normally never came from or from inside me. Because though I was feeling good after meeting Akash and I rather wanted to dance, I was trying to suppress my emotions. I entered my room and looked at my phone, it was one in the night already, there were two missed calls from Sahil and a message which said, "Hey don't call me back. I will be sleeping, need to get up early."

CHAPTER 18

I was super excited the next day after meeting Akash. I was all smiles in the hospital. "Wow, Vaani is a little more enthusiastic and happy today than her usual self," said Shivani. She really liked me and I really liked her, and to her comment instead of saying anything I showed her my teeth and gave her a big smile. "Oh my God, what has happened?" she asked. I smiled again and said, "Nothing madam. You should also be happy for no reason like this." Akash had told me not to tell people in the organization about us being friends. According to him, people in the organization needed reasons to talk about others and he did not want to give them any topic of gossips. I partly agreed to that and then because he was more experienced than I was so I chose to follow his advice. But it was too difficult not to narrate our meeting to anyone. So I chose my two buddies, Sahil and Manav over the others around me. Sahil was busy at work and so I spoke to Manav first, "Hello, it's me!" "Oh I see, is it my personal banker from ICICI bank?" He said. We tried to say our hellos in a different way each time we spoke. After those tiny light talks with him, I started off with my narration about the previous day's dinner. "It was so good, Manav, all windy and nice. I enjoyed his company and had a good time. And you won't believe I slept at some three but I am still all fresh." He listened to my entire narration patiently and said, "I don't know but I feel you shouldn't indulge a lot in him." "Please man! I am so happy and you are just putting your mind in between." "Not that," he continued, "see you are a very work-oriented person. And I want you to focus on your ambitions. Don't be like the others Vaani. I know you have started earning so you feel more independent but then please have your schedule right. All this just worsens over the period of days that's why I am saying" I heard his lecture with a partly deaf ear and assured him that nothing was happening to my schedule and then I always have my focus right on work and my principals right in place. Later that evening I made the same narration to Sahil. He was different, his confidence in me was different, perhaps because he knew me for over many years. He was too happy to know that I was finally feeling settled in the city and I had some good company to hang out with. "It was good man, Sahil. The music, the place, all so lively with cool young crowd, unlike in our place where all we have are eve-teasers." I said. "Hmm, yes. Enjoy the differences and these are new experiences all together. I am glad you get to see so many different things and people," was his reaction to it. No doubt he was the perfect friend that anyone would want.

A week later during some conversation over messages that me and Akash were having, he sent me some pictures of a place near his home where he was relishing his beer, and watching the cricket match. It was IPL season and the Hyderabadis were going crazy for Sun Risers Hyderabad. And since no team from Uttar Pradesh existed, even I was supporting the same. "You are too sweet," popped a message and my usual blushing started. "So are you," I replied. "Nah I am not," he said and before I could finish typing my reply, "Mom" flashed on my screen. My mother and I did not have regular conversations. We were more in touch through Whatsapp messages. "Yes hello mummy." I started, and we spoke about some routine things. I flaunted at how people were liking me at my workplace and how I was planning my savings each month from my salary etc. In between while I was talking I started getting another call. I saw it was Akash, I was least expecting his call because he was outside with his friends somewhere for dinner. I continued to speak to my mother and thought I will call him back once I am done talking to her, but within a minute I started getting a call from him again. I told my mother that I will call her later and answered his call. "Always busy on phone madam," he sounded a little louder than usual as he seemed to be driving his bike. "Party over! So soon *haan*." I said, "I will be there at your place in another fifteen minutes." "My place?" "Ya, why not?" "Stop kidding me." I laughed. "I am serious, I will be there," he said and hung up. Mad guy, I said in my head. I called my mother again and finished my conversation with her. Akash's place was at the other end of the city from where I stayed. We resided at the north and south poles and in between us was a long stretch of approximately thirty kilometers. So I obviously did not take him seriously. After speaking to her I got back to doing my routine things. I was sorting some things in my handbag when he called again. I smiled and answered, "What happened?" "I am right outside your building." "No." I said, "Come down fast." My heart started thumping a little more than usual and I hurried out in my balcony to see if he was actually there because it was hard to believe that he could drive down just to meet me. I looked down and saw him on his bike. "Whaaat!" I screamed over the phone, "I am coming." I said and hung up. I quickly changed from my casual pajamas to an informal jeans and a simple t-shirt and ran as fast as I could. It was around ten thirty in the night. Most of the accommodation girls were probably sleeping as the corridors were quiet and even the guard was fast asleep. I opened the main gate and went out near his bike where he stood all in smiles. "You are actually here, Oh my God! Look at you." "Why will I joke?" He said. I was blushing again and moving front, back and sideways in excitement rather than standing still. "Why are you moving back and forth? Don't run, I am not going to do anything to you," he chuckled. "Yes I mean, oh am I moving? I didn't realize." I uttered some confusing words, because it was hard to believe that he had driven so much at that time of the night just to see me. "I cancelled a plan at my friends place and I rather thought that it was better to come here and see you." "Oh I am too good you see," I smiled. "I know, that's why I am here." He got down from his bike and we just stood there and spoke about many common things again. He asked me some silly medical questions like a typical senior to test my knowledge, and gave me some tips about the organization for which we both were working. "I am supposed to return my friend some money," he said. And took out a lot of cash from his pocket. "Help me count it." He handed over the bundle to me. It was some fifty odd thousand rupees. "Wow, you are carrying so much cash." I was amazed. "It's all yours," he lit a cigarette, looked at me and smiled. I did not know what it meant. Do boys say such things even when they do not really like the other person, or is it that he was too much into me I thought. Or maybe it's just the alcohol talking I explained myself. Engrossed in those thoughts while I counted the money I dropped a note on the ground, "Oops sorry," I bent down to pick up the fallen note and handed over the rest of the bundle to him. "But that's not the way to say sorry," he continued to blow some smoke out of his mouth. "Oh, then?" I asked. "You don't know how to say sorry?" He asked me and I stared at him blankly to which he extended his arms and raised an eyebrow. Unlike the previous time when he had gestured the same and I looked confused, this time I understood that it was a call for a hug. And unlike the previous time when I was rather conscious this time I went ahead a little more confidently and hugged him and to my surprise there was no reciprocation from his side at all. He just continued to take a puff of his cigarette. "Sorry," I stood back. "Nah! That was nothing. It should be a tighter hug," he said. "I see, now how do you do that when the other person doesn't even reciprocate?" I argued. "You want me to show you how to do that?" "You can," I said. He threw his cigarette aside and within no time lifted me some feet above the ground, holding me tightly and very close to him which took me by surprise. I had no clue about what had happened and I didn't know where to go. I held him lightly around his neck and shied away from looking at him while he continued to stare at me straight into my eyes. "Look at me," he said, and I turned my head. "Look at me for a minute," he said again. While he continued to hold me in the same manner, I looked at him and I looked at him like I never looked at anyone before. There was sudden surge of mixed emotions that passed inside me. After that we still spoke for quite some time, but my mind was blocked. I did not know what was happening. He held me by my waist for the rest of the time that we spoke that night. And right before leaving, he gave me a little peck on my cheek and forwarded his own towards me. "What?" I said. "Your turn, I also want one," he demanded. And held me again, I touched his cheeks lightly from my lips. "Nah it's not considered until we get a kissing sound." He had held me tightly and the only option I had to let him go was to try again. I gave him another peck and tried making a kissing sound to which he smiled, left me and wore his helmet. "See you again soon," he waved at me and left. I went back to my room to find that I had left my phone inside and I didn't even realize it. This came to me as a surprise because just like anyone else now a day's even I fell under the category of people who check their phone all the time. It was almost one in the night which again took me by surprise because we stood and spoke for some good two and a half hours outside a building which seemed just nothing. I had a couple of missed calls. Sahil, Manav, my sister and one unknown number. I couldn't call anyone back that late at night. Lost in my own thoughts I was just trying to figure what had just happened in the past couple of hours and how and why was I being with him the way I was. All that I could think was that maybe this was a new me. Maybe this was my new side which I had neither seen nor explored before.

CHAPTER 19

I had begun to feel gradual changes in myself. I was no more in my strict schedule, I used to skip my breakfast more often because I never got up on time. I was less tensed about anything happening in the hospital, I was becoming a greater techno-freak. Unlike how I was, a simple living girl with no interest in brands or tags, now I wanted them all. And yes, unlike previously I had very less time for Sahil and Manav. I wasn't sharing anything and everything with them about Akash because they had their objections to make. Shivani was my new support for this. Though I filtered out what I told her, but then yes, it used to relieve me a lot from what I was feeling then. I had strictly told her not to tell anyone else about we two being friends and she was completely supportive. I felt happy with Akash and I couldn't dare to put up any inhibitions on myself. The usual me was always tied up with a narrow band of restrictions around, the usual me always knew what my limitations were and where I needed to control or stop myself. But I don't know from where the new me got the courage to break all my inhibitions and go where the instinct was taking it. I never imagined that I could cross all my barriers until someday in one of my meetings with Akash sometime in May, May eleventh to be precise.

"Me bored, thinking to go for some movie." I messaged him. It was a week off for me and I was lazing in my room since the morning. I usually spent my week offs watching some or the other movie. I never bothered about company; in fact most of the times I used to treat myself with a ticket for gold lounge in the theatre, lay down get some coke and garlic bread and enjoy the movie. "What time?" he asked, "I am still looking for some show timings. There is a nice Hindi movie playing featuring Mr. Bachchan." "Check after six-thirty, I will join you," was the reply I got immediately. Wow, I got some company. I was elated and booked a seven thirty show in a theatre near both of us. I spent the rest of my day washing some clothes and re-arranging the shelves which happened to be my favorite tasks then. I had kept the door and windows of my room open to let some fresh air in, and from the open doors came two tiny kids who apparently stayed in my accommodation. One was the guards daughter and the other was the owners daughter, "*Akka*, give me your phone I want to take a picture" said one of them, they called me *Akka,* a word which is usually used to address elder sisters in the southern portion of India. Phone for pictures! I wondered how the games and entertainment had changed for kids over a period of years. I mean I think it was when I was in school that the first mobile phone had come in the Indian market and us siblings thought that it was a very big thing and never touched the one in our family. How rapidly it progressed, and how rapidly the technology grew till today when a five-year-old was asking me for my own mobile phone to take some pictures. "Do you even know how to take pictures kiddo?" I tapped lightly on her head, "Yes *Akka,* give me please, just two minutes *Akka,*" she pulled my pajama and made a sad face to which I laughed and gave her the phone. To my surprise she was very well versed with the buttons, she knew where the camera was and she straight away went to that application, whereas meanwhile, the other kid posed like a supermodel for some candid shots. I laughed, I clapped and I whistled at the live show going on and had a light time with them until one of their mothers came looking for them, pulled their ear and took them to sleep. It was almost five thirty in the evening and I realized that even I needed to wind up the mess which I had created in my room and start getting ready for my movie outing.

It doesn't matter how many times a girl has met someone before, even if it's for the nth time trust me I feel she is equally conscious in dressing up, irrespective of whom she is going to meet. And then when it's some guy that she hangs out with on and off then, of course, the efforts increase a little. Brands are what Akash was crazy about and I had a handful of branded clothes in my wardrobe so choosing one wasn't a difficult task. This time I just planned to accessorize it a little differently, over the ink blue top that I wore I put up a heavy chain which was long and looked very fashionable. So there I was, ready for the day; neither over, nor underdressed, looked at myself in the mirror made my hair fall on my forehead a little more than usual to add some special effects, smiled at my overall look and pushed out for the movie.

This time I was there at the theatre before Akash reached and I was glad about it because that gave me some time to settle, and then he never liked it if I reached late. So I tried my best to make it before him. It was a Sunday evening and the place was quite crowded. Some were rushing to buy last moment tickets for the movie; some were dragging their kids to eat something in the food court which was there on the same floor and some young couples were wandering aimlessly who seemed to be just looking around and having a good time. My phone rang and it was Akash. "Yes I am outside the movie entrance already." I answered. "I can see you, I am somewhere around." Oops! I thought and started looking around in a hurry, while I simultaneously made sure that my hair was in place and my accessories hadn't moved. "Stop checking out all the men out there lady," he chuckled; I blushed and found him straight in front of me. My smile always widened when I was with him and with the same gesture I moved towards him. Unlike the previous times when we usually shook hands on meeting this time he put his hand around my neck like an old buddy and patted on my head. It was seven thirty already so we did not talk much and just rushed into the theatre and took our seats. I had booked two corner seats in the third row, it being a Sunday and with the same day booking the third row was a luxury for Mr. Bachchan's movie because the rest of the upper seats were pre-booked two-three days in advance. Watching movies in the city was the cheapest and best time pass, no matter which day of the week it was and which row we were booking. It was a flat one hundred and fifty rupees for the ticket unlike in other big cities where it had wide variations. We barely spoke while the movie played, except if he wanted to ask the meaning of some Hindi word which our Mr. South Indian did not understand. The show got over by around tenish and because both of us hadn't had our dinner he decided to take me to a small restaurant behind the theatre to have some yummy *desi paranthas.* It was a dingy, tiny restaurant where everyone seemed to know him and it looked like he was a regular there. Meanwhile, till the dinner was served the waiter got him a cigarette; I assumed that he was regular there with his cigarettes as well. He began to smoke while we had our little talks. I told him tits and bits about my family over dinner, about how my sister was married in a different culture and how much fun the wedding was and so on and so forth. In the middle of the meal the electricity went off and the waiter lit up a candle between us. I had my first candlelight experience in that tiny and dingy eatery, but I was elated. Since it was late already so without wasting much time we settled our bills fast and pushed out.

Akash drove me back and stood outside my accommodation entrance for some time. "I am too tired to drive back, my house is a good twenty kilometers or more from here," he yawned. We both stayed in two separate ends of the city and that was the main reason why we planned our outings less often. I guess if we stayed near we would have seen each other almost every day. "Never mind, all you need to do once you get back is sleep. So consider this as one final work for the day and drive back," I smiled. "I will just stay back at your place," he looked at me with tired eyes. "It's a girls accommodation," I showed him the board. "Doesn't matter I will sneak in," he made a tired face again. "Sneak inside! Please there are CCTV cameras throughout and it's not allowed." "Who sees the cameras? It's going to be fine. Empathize with my situation. I have worked throughout the day, drove almost forty kilometers on a bike already. I will go early in the morning. No one will even notice me," he tried to convince me. "Fine even if you come where will you sleep, my room is very small with a single bed and I don't have an extra bedding either," his energy reappeared from somewhere and he said. "Balcony, floor anywhere." I argued for some ten more minutes but he failed to listen. I had never done anything so daring in my life before, irrespective of the cameras or the guard, getting a man inside my accommodation was something beyond my imagination. It was almost twelve in the night, I opened the main door as slowly as I could and walked up through the stairs because there was no elevator in the building. I found that the corridors were empty, the doors were closed, and the lights were turned off except for the dim ones in the passages. I gave him a call as soon as I reached up, told him to sneak in through the open entrance and guided him the way up to my room. And there he was, with me, in my room.

I hadn't switched on the lights because I was scared if someone would have noticed us and I was scared that someone would come and catch me with a male inside the building. Within no time he put his bag aside and laid down on the single bed which I had in my room. "I am scared," I whispered. "It's ok, sit here," he moved aside a little and gave me some space in my own bed. I sat and wondered if he had any plans to leave my bed. Considering he was my guest for the night I got up and said, "You be comfortable here, I will curl up on the floor." He held my hand and made me sit beside him, moved his hand to my waist, "Any guy can die for the waist you have," he said and in a sudden jerk, got up, held me tightly and came over me to kiss me. I resisted but gave up soon. For the next five minutes we smooched. It came too naturally to me and I don't know how. His hands slid around my waist and then moved up over my chest. The old me was resisting and was simultaneously stunned to see all that was happening, the principled young girl whose life revolved only around work and who was untouched and unaffected by any boy like this was fading away. The new me, on the other hand, was giving up on the resistance, the new me was justifying everything that was happening, the new me just surrendered completely to the young man that she was with.

We laid together on the same narrow bed, he took the pillow while I rested on his arm for the rest of the night. He held me tightly and dozed off soon. I don't think I had ever felt that close to anyone in my life before. While I was still smiling at myself, I got disturbed by some sudden light from my phone. It was Sahil's call. I did not accept or reject the call, just took the phone and kept it deep in my handbag.

CHAPTER 20

So here it was the always cautious and sensible me, had fallen for someone who claimed that he was super casual. But why and how? When I always carried my brain on my sleeve and took any step after thinking more than a thousand times. Was it because I felt that he was the kind of guy I always fantasized for, was it because he was super bold with me which no one else had ever been in the past, or was it because somewhere we had a connection which could just not be explained.

Next day Akash left my accommodation early in the morning without anyone noticing him and I felt relieved. Though I was on cloud nine after that, I was equally lost. I didn't realize it unless others started to point it. "Madam is looking like she is in some other world today," commented my receptionist in the hospital. Oops! I got careful. I didn't know it shows on your face. I was checking my phone repeatedly to see if Akash had messaged me. I had all sorts of thoughts in my mind. What if he will never talk to me again, what if he thought that I wasn't a good girl; had I given up too easily for him? But then I thought everything came so naturally last night, it came out of affection for him, no I was not wrong. I kept explaining to myself again and again. The worst was that I was alone in this battle of thoughts; it was something I couldn't tell anyone, it was something I couldn't even tell the usual keeper of all my secrets Sahil. In the pool of thoughts it was those rare times when I kept all to myself, no talking to Shivani, no calling anyone, just did my work and sat with the newspaper staring at it blankly. It was almost two in the afternoon and there was still no news from him, I opened my message box and typed, "Hey, how have you been? I hope you reached last..." Nah! I deleted it and kept my phone aside. I don't know why but I wanted him to message me first. I guess it was just to assure that he was fine with me after all that happened between us last night. Perhaps I was embarrassed and so I just wanted to be sure that we were still the same.

Late in the afternoon at around three finally, my message beeped and yes it was him. All of a sudden I started speaking to Shivani about something that she was telling me so as to just preserve the treasure before finally opening it. "Hey cutie! I got up now lolz! Am rushing to the hospital." Wow. For a second I could relate to how the pressure cookers might be feeling as their first whistle goes off! I was so relieved to finally hear from him, "Lazy boy, I already did a lot of work here since morning." "You are so impressive, me the laziest, and by the way, could you still see me while you were doing all your work?" He winked at that. "Don't ask!!!" I responded. I came back to my usual self after that little conversation from him and then he pushed off for work and I engrossed myself in some too.

A few days later it was Manav's birthday. I remember the previous year I had sat online for almost twenty days every day and discussed with people to look for some present that I could give him. Along with a power bank for on the go charging I got a pretty cake delivered for him made of KitKat and gems like how they do it for kids. Two faced Gemini is what I always called him; I was a sun sign freak whereas Manav had no clue what it meant until of course, he met me. "I am Gemini, so it means I am helpful and easily bored and creative," he used to laugh initially and only later he gave up and became a firm believer in the traits that are mentioned for each sign. This year was different. I didn't sit searching for anything at all for his special day because lost in my own new world I completely forgot that his birthday was around the corner. Thanks to some social networking site where I was notified about the day; when I called to wish him the first thing that he said was, "Your parcel is late! I already ate my cake!" I had been spending a lot of money on my outings with Akash, and I was saving some to gift him an I-pod on his birthday, so I had decided to cut down on Manav's birthday present that year. Poor Manav was hopeful that my little parcel must be stuck somewhere and he'll get it in a day or two. But I am not sure where the poor me was. Because his words, his hope nothing affected me at all, "it's ok I thought, why do we need to send presents each year."

But perhaps it's not about the presents; it's not about the material things ever and at all. We deliver gifts, cakes, flowers and other little things to show that we care. Love needs to be expressed, relationship needs to be nurtured, affection needs to be reciprocated, it's because if we don't take care of people and take them for granted then things start falling apart.

CHAPTER 21

In the days to come there were no serious discussions between me and Akash, be it on relationships, or on the intimacy between us. Things were just the same, we hung out together for movies and for dinners after which he either used to drop me back or stay back with me. I was more confident in letting him into the girl's accommodation unlike before. More than my confidence, I developed a sense of trust in him that whatever it was he will take care. We both used to enjoy the time that we spent with each other and stayed connected through endless messages and phone calls in the times when we were not together.

Once unlike the usual night movies, we met on the first-day first show, of a new Hindi movie that was put up. And because our Mr. Handsome wanted to be the first one to see it, we booked the nine AM show in a theatre near his home. My plan was to get up early, watch the movie, take a cab after it got over and travel back to my place. I dressed up very simply in my regular *salwar kameez* and a tiny bindi on my forehead because I was supposed to attend the hospital duties after the show. This time we booked the last row purposely so that we don't have people behind us and we could be freer with each other, and yes we did behave like one of those couples in the movie theatre, holding hands and resting on each other's shoulders. After the movie was over I opened my phone to book a cab but Akash suggested that he would drop me till some nearby common point from where I could take a regular city bus. His idea seemed alright to me because the cab would have taken a long time to come so I hopped on his bike and covered my head and face with my dupatta to avoid the mid-day sun. The old city was more crowded and dusty unlike the newer portion of the city where I stayed, but he was swift in crossing the narrow lanes or the heavy traffic. "Listen where should I drop you?" He asked me. "How would I know, you said there is a bus station nearby right?" I said. To which I realized that perhaps he never knew of any station nearby and he just wanted to spend a little more time with me while we drove. That was quite typical of him, he never expressed anything openly. "We'll go home, I have some work and you can see my place as well." What! I thought in my head and immediately turned on my front camera to see how horrible I was looking to meet his family for the first time. "No, no how can I come to your place like this," was my response, "I mean what will your parents think, and look at my clothes, drop me here please. I will take an auto." "Shut up, we are going." He turned his bike into a narrow lane, and there I was in front of a yellow building with two floors where the black and white name board outside the house read as Mr. Mahantesh Salian, who was his father.

The drawing room was where I entered first. It was a rectangular room with a low-lying bed, some sofas, and a rocking chair, there were two cupboards with glass doors which had his father's books and some old audio cassettes which unfortunately the current generation is far away from because all the music is readily available either on the phones or over the internet. The collection of books looked classic. I could see some religious books and some philosophical non-fiction books by renowned authors, very old pictures, and some classic old showpieces were neatly arranged and kept. Where do we find it in today's world I thought, the world was busier in replacing and throwing the old and bringing some fast and fancy things which didn't last. I can live here forever I wanted to tell him but while I was having a look at the shelf someone interrupted me from behind and said, "His father is a voracious reader," it was his mother, she greeted me warmly. I smiled at her and introduced myself. We sat in the drawing room and spoke about each other's states and families for some time till Akash finished his work at home. After which his mother showed me around and then got busy in cooking something. Besides the drawing room in the house there were three other rooms, a kitchen, and a common space. He took me to his room and before I could even look around, he held me tightly and kissed me. I felt elated, I felt like we were married and were having a private encounter hiding from his mother in his own house. In a hurry burry after that, I saw some of his childhood pictures which hung on the wall in his room. He looked like a cute and naughty child. He tried holding me again but I ran to the kitchen to talk to his mother, but he dragged me halfway because both of us were getting late for our work. Later that evening he messaged me, "Did you like my tiny house?" Of course, I did! It was full of warmth and values, I wanted to tell him that I had loved it just the way I loved him but then I was not too good in expressing either and just said a small, "Yes of course!"

Actually more than expressing love to each other we needed to talk and discuss ourselves with each other. We needed to speak about our relationship, and about where exactly we were heading with it. But then though we were running in our thirties, unfortunately, we were driven like teenagers. We were just blindly flowing with our feelings without knowing or thinking about the consequences and the emotional turmoil that the future was holding for us.

CHAPTER 22

Once while having some casual conversation Akash asked me if I would want to accompany him to the Tirupati temple. Tirupati is one of the most renowned religious places across the country and I had never gone there. The journey he said was overnight from the private travel buses. He had to attend some conference in that city and so he planned to go with me, visit the temple and the next day attend the session he wanted to. "And how about the stay?" I was curious to know. "I have a friend who works in a hotel I will get a room booked for both of us," he told me. Room! I thought in my head, I mean yes by now I was bold enough to let him in my accommodation but then staying somewhere outside and booking a room to ourselves still needed some courage. While I was wondering about it, he said: "The place is good and safe so you will not have any problems even when you are there the next day all by yourself while I go to attend the conference." Of course, I trusted him with the place but I needed to gather some courage to plan a trip like this with him. Outside India young girls and boys do go out and stay together, but here in India there were so many things that could have come in between. Legal issues of an unmarried couple staying together, some random relatives that you may bump into who will end up questioning you a thousand things and so on and so forth. But then whenever Akash asked me something, I just couldn't deny it. Why? I had stopped asking that to myself because I knew I did not have an answer. So after the usual little tug of thoughts, I agreed to accompany him. He said he would book the tickets and confirm the dates at the earliest. And as usual, some shopping followed for the trip thereafter. I never left any stone unturned to look my best for Akash. In fact, there were days when I used to buy new clothes on the go just to meet him. I had never been that lavish in my life ever, but then I had never been the way I was being with him either.

We were supposed to leave on a Friday from a pickup point near my house at six in the evening, which meant that I would have to leave the hospital a good three hours before my usual timing. I was quite excited to wind up my work early and soon after lunch, my excitement reached greater heights. There was no message or call from Akash during the daytime because we both wanted to be free early from work. I hadn't told anyone around about where I was going because of the usual feeling of thief inside the burglar. I just said that my brother was visiting Bangalore and I had to be with him for the weekend to show him around. The moment the clock showed five I rushed out like Cinderella but since the pickup point was just five minutes away from my accommodation. I had some spare time and I dozed off as soon as I reached my place. I got up only when Akash called me to ask my whereabouts. "Come fast mad girl, you are sleeping! I don't believe this," he shouted. Oops! I got up fast, did some last moment packing and rushed out to take the bus, to meet him.

"Item," he smiled and greeted me with a warm hug as we met. It was always such a pleasure to meet him and now when we were actually going to travel together I was feeling very different. He was dressed up in his casual gray t-shirt and loose jogging pants and was sporting a rugged look as always which I loved. Even I was in my in formals, a cropped-jacket and a loose pair of jeans is what I wore. Both of us did not have much luggage either except for two small bag packs that we were carrying. We looked like one of those hippie travelers. A small pick up bus took us to the main bus station; we sat on the last seat of the small and crowded pickup bus. Akash was as happy as I was about the travel; he never said that but gestured all the same. He was talking more than usual and showing the best of his affection. On our way, we crossed some posh localities of the city with skyscrapers and really beautiful buildings. "I love this, I will have a house in one of those someday soon," he held me and said. "I will tell you many things about myself on this trip which I have never told you before. You know if you want to practice Dentistry in Australia then there is a certain exam that you have to qualify." Why Australia all of a sudden! I thought, but then because he was in the flow of talking so I did not interrupt him. We had booked a sleeper bus to travel for convenience, the berths in the bus were just like they have in a train compartment four separate bunker berths in one coupe. Akash and I had the parallel ones on top. Instead of going to our respective seats we curled up together on one of the seats till the dinner break. He opened up quite a lot to me, he told me more about his family, his father, how work was treating him and so on and so forth. Even I told him a lot of things about how I was, my family, my friends, about Sahil and Manav and how they had always stood for me. We had never spoken so much about each other's lives before.

The next day morning we landed in God's land, Tirupati, *Devasthala* is what they call it. Our hotel was straight in front of where the bus had dropped us and so we walked our way to the place. Fortunately, no one at the reception asked us any questions and we straight away checked into the room. It was a decent four-star hotel and the rooms were posh and big. The housekeeping people accompanied us to the room to show us the basic things and the moment they left we both looked at each other in a moment of ecstasy because we were finally somewhere in private since the time we had met. Akash dosed off for some time and I started getting ready. We had to walk up the seven hills and so we started early. We chose to walk up barefoot. It was a beautiful place and the weather was just perfect for the day; a little cloudy and windy.

In front of us were steps which were painted yellow and red in some places. As we moved up the steps continued as well. In some places, they were shallow and easier to climb while in the other places they got steep and tiring. There were many people who were climbing up with us, people of different age groups and people with different ways of devotion. There were some who were walking up entirely on their knees, some who were putting a little red dot on each step as they climbed, some who were chit-chatting and taking frequent breaks in between, while some who chanted mantras and continued to just walk. It was beautiful to see so many different forms of devotees who wanted to walk up to reach the same destination, to feel the same power of God. Akash and I were talking and taking little breaks. Since he was a smoker, his lungs did not permit him to walk up constantly. There were small little shops and vendors on the way selling water and little edibles so that the devotees could be comfortable with the basic facilities. In the middle of somewhere we crossed an area with deer around us. Akash told me that there was a dense forest that surrounded the area and that is why the steps were blocked on either side with fences. He used to visit the place once every year and so he was briefing me about everything on the way. Everyone just continued to move with the same devotion chanting "*Govinda*" on the way for hours together. It was certainly a walk to remember.

It was not before eleven in the night that we finally entered the temple premises close to God's idol, the chanting became louder and the crowd got bigger; Akash kept his hands on my shoulder from behind and kept directing me and protecting me from passers-by. "Join your hands, keep your eyes wide open and look towards the right," he said as we passed the place where from a distance we saw the idol of God. It was serene, and the place definitely had some strong vibes. More than anything else I was happy to see the way they had maintained the decorum and cleanliness of the place despite so many devotees visiting the temple. Only the priests stayed near the idol and the rest of us just walked around and said our prayers. In my portion of the country all the devotees are usually allowed to go near the idol in most of the temples. In fact, on certain occasions, all individual devotees offer things like water, milk, flowers, and sweets for the idol. In a country where the resources were depleting and hygiene needed to be maintained, I never supported it. After the *darshan,* we took a bus to go back to our hotel. Akash had some muscle cramps and he had to attend the conference on the following day so he made me eat something from the hotel and slept off. I looked at him for quite some time before I slept that night. The way he had cared about little things throughout the day had touched me deeply. With all my heart I did want to marry this man someday. I sneaked in the same blanket as his, held him and slept after the thoughts in my mind rested.

I spent the next day all by myself. I watched some movie, ordered some pizza and in no time he was back and it was time for us to leave the city. We shared some happy moments in our room before we finally left the place. On our way back in the bus Akash wasn't talking as much as he was on our onward journey. Somehow I didn't want to sleep that night, because I knew that when I will get up we'll part again and get busy with our works. "Talk to me man, as it is our trip is getting over. Keep your phone aside no," I kept telling him. "Look here," he called me to his side of the berth to show me something on his phone. "How is this girl?" He asked me. "She is fine, as in who is she and why are you asking?" I was curious to know. "She is from one of our known families in Mumbai. My parents really like her, they want me to get married to her." He said. For a second I just froze, marry her? I thought in my mind but then I controlled myself and asked, "But how about you?" "She is good, she will surely take good care of me and my family, and then I am planning to move to Australia in a couple of months and she is ok to relocate. But then I am still having some second thoughts," he said. I felt broken. I never knew what it meant to feel that way but I did feel broken at that point of time. He was moving abroad and he never told me about it all this while was one thought, and who was I then was the other. I had submitted myself completely to this man who actually comprised my life. But then what was I for him, I wondered? I was surprised how it never occurred to me before and I was surprised that he was so casual to tell me about the proposal that he was thinking about. My eyes welled up, I wanted to cry loudly but I held myself and my tears. Thankfully Akash continued to stare at his phone and did not notice my emotions. I did not want to be mocked at, I did not want to tell how I felt to someone whom I thought may not even relate to it. "Oh is it! But you never told me that you will move, and then what about me? You'll leave me alone?" I asked him as normally as I could, "It never occurred to me to tell you lady, and then who is leaving you alone. I always tell you everything about myself, somehow we gel so well. I will always stay connected, you are one of my closest friends," he said while he continued to message someone over the phone. Close yes I was in all forms I thought. I had heard a phrase called 'friends with benefits' over the internet many times and that day I could see one in myself. I was completely blank from within; I told him that I needed to get some sleep and quietly moved to my berth. Once again there were a millions of thoughts which crowded in my mind. Rather than looking at him this night I wanted to look at my own face and ask myself where I was truly headed with him. But ironically my idiotic self, defended all my questions and doubts yet again. My idiotic self said that he does like me and he is just inexpressive. I decided to give him his own time and space, it was a divine connection my heart said and once again and I failed to prove him wrong and slept in peace.

CHAPTER 23

The next day after I reached my accommodation, I had mixed thoughts. The happiness, and the thrill of the trip was diluted by the conversation we had the previous night. I had defended all doubts against him very well to my own self, but there were certain questions which had crept into my mind. I had to rush to work and so instead of thinking about it a thousand times over I quickly had my breakfast, took bath, changed and went for work.

I was a workaholic for sure and I am glad that I was because it shields you from all the other unnecessary thoughts. If I would have been in my accommodation I may have had gray hair thinking about how casual Akash was last night, and whether he ever liked me or not. It is funny though that if people really mean to us, then no matter how many times they hurt us, no matter what their attitude is towards us we end up defending them, protecting them and forgiving them for whatever they do. "Madam, the head of our neighbouring office has come over for treatment and they want you to perform the treatment that is needed." I was interrupted by my receptionist. "Yes please arrange for a checkup and treatment, make him seated in the VIP lounge and I will be there," I said. I was never in favor to treat patients like VIPs. When the disease is the same and the procedures are the same then everyone deserves to be attended equally and dealt with equally. But I guess people in the corporate hospital setups did not think like me. In fact, everywhere in every field, things are just the same. We make certain people out of a huge lot the important ones, we discriminate them either because of the money they possess or the power they have. We create and promote inequalities ourselves and then we protest for equality. I was getting philosophical, maybe because this was a buffer to my background thoughts about Akash. Anyways, I did not want to lose my job and so I went ahead with the protocols, put up a wide smile on my face and received Mr. VIP for treatment. It was a busy day for me thereafter and so I was completely occupied and had no time to think anything else till our lunch break. I and Shivani always had lunch together, I loved the way she cooked *dal,* everyone in Andhra, in fact, was just perfect at cooking *sambar* or *dal,* they cooked it so well that I could never resist it ever. I used to pack the usual lunch which my accommodation mess provided, but we shared each other's food, ordered some pickle and curd to add to the grandeur of our meals every day. "So how is it going in the city for you Vaani? I believe you have made too many friends here. It just doesn't appear that you are not one of us. It looks like you belong to this city itself, you have mixed up so well with everyone," she said and smiled at me, the one person whom I thought I will always have in my fan club was Shivani. She loved me just the way I was and that is why I was always so comfortable sharing anything and everything with her. "Good madam, you know I visited Akash's house some time back," she looked at me in surprise. "You did! Wow great, you people have become best buddies I believe." "Yes we get along very well madam, and he keeps making plans with me every now and then." "Hmm...it means he wants you to be around, he may be enjoying your company," she looked internally happy to say that. "Oh yes, he told me that even he was surprised how we gel so well and then he confides in me for many things as well." Yes he did and I was proud to say that because Akash always had a very different image of not opening up to people so easily because of some past which even I did not know about. But like how every workplace has a rumor for someone or the other, in our organization people said that he used to really love someone a few years back and then because of something that went wrong between them he was always casual about relationships and never took anything seriously except his work. In fact, some senior colleagues who knew him for longer criticized him and told other people not to hang out with him, whom they called as the crazy guy. I never gave an ear to all those. I always believed what I saw. He was good to me and he was good at his work and that was all that mattered to me. Shivani smiled again and just kept looking at me for a minute. "What!" I blushed. "Are you sure it's just friendship?" She continued to smile and I continued to blush. Both of us knew it wasn't just being friends, everyone around could see it then why not him, I wondered.

I was just glancing through some messages in my phone that night when Sahil called me, "Nowadays you are in your own world, no calls, no messages nothing," he complained. "It's me who calls you all the time, Sahil. I wanted to see if you would call me when I don't," was my clever reply. "In that case, see I called you." "Yes you are always great," was my response. He had called me at a point when my mind was just struggling to come out of Akash's thoughts and my mind was tired of the battle that was going on inside it against him. I always had the habit to tell Sahil everything about my life, but I never dared to tell him the details about my relationship with Akash. At this point in time, I wanted to pour out everything to him. I started, "Akash and I ..." and started coughing rather loudly, there was no irritant in my throat but an inhibition in my brain which stopped me from telling it all to him. Such inhibitions of the brain are usually called as being disloyal. Yes, of course, I was being one, but I always had a logical explanation to prove this wrong side of mine right. Anyways, I just made up for the sudden cough and once again decided to talk to him partially and diplomatically about the entire situation. "Hey, do you think Akash is not that good or something?" I asked him. "He is your friend, you will know him more than I do." "Hmm yes but I don't know Sahil, sometimes he is too sweet, sometimes he is aloof. I am so confused. I don't know what exactly does he feel for me. I am not sure if he likes me or not." "Wait! Why are you mixing your friendship with so many emotional pressures and expectations Vaani?" He said. "Stay normal and let him be the way he is." "Yes that is true but then I don't know why I get so possessive about people. If he doesn't talk I feel insecure," I explained. "Relax! Don't overthink about things. People do have their mood swings and they do have their priorities so just chill tiny tot." Hmm...his words made sense but why wasn't I able to say it open and loud to him. I was getting insecure and possessive because I had fallen in love with him. "Anyways how come you are awake till so late?" I asked him. "It's my night duty today and there are many sick kids in my ward," he told. "Half of them are suffering from a disease of the liver called *Wilsons disease,* and the specific medicine which is needed for its treatment is not available in the Indian market at all! I don't know what's wrong! I have tried my best to find out why it is not available but I am not able to. Children's parents come to us and constantly tell us that their child's health is deteriorating but all that we can do is, write the prescription and send them to find if they can get the medicine from somewhere. But we also know it isn't available. I have contacted my paediatric colleagues all across the country and they say it's nowhere. I haven't felt this helpless in my life for anything ever. I see the children dying Vaani and I can't do anything about it. I have written a petition, I have posted in the social media about it, I just want someone in power to read it and help me and help the kids." My heart sank! He was such a noble soul. Most of us want to learn in order to achieve, to get name, fame, and money but all that was far from even touching Sahil. He learned to help others, he learned so that he could create a difference in their lives. Years back we both had similar thoughts and similar ambitions and it was these which had driven us together from acquaintances to best friends. But unlike me, he was persistent and determined, he was not driven by everything that came in his way, he knew the true value of relationships. With the instinctive attitude which I was carrying at that point in time, I was happily sailing in the boat of disloyalty and lies. The strong winds of truth and honesty were trying to stop me on my way, but I failed to get affected and I failed to foresee my downfall and I just happily kept sailing.

CHAPTER 24

What happened next came as a shocker to me, and it woke me up from the dream world in which I had been till now. It was a few months later that year when things were running smoothly between me and Akash, work was just fine and I was completely engrossed in the city and its culture. I was roaming in a mall for some window shopping on my day off from work when my phone rang, it was Sahil. I was surprised by his call because it was one in the afternoon and it was an odd time for him to call. Afternoons used to be his peak working hours. I was wondering why he could have called and received his call. “Vaani!” he sounded much louder and much more thrilled than his usual self. I was worried now. “Guess what babe?” Babe! Wow, he never called me babe. I was sure something big had happened. With a thumping heart and alert ears I asked him, “Hey what happened man?” I sounded more tensed than excited. “It seems your parents had visited my house yesterday, why didn’t you tell me that? Were you intending to surprise me?” “What! When, I did not know that myself!” “You didn’t know! I am surprised! Madam your parents were in my hometown yesterday for some work and they planned a sudden visit to my house. They took the address from my elder brother over the phone whose number they already had, and they went and met my father." I was astonished, while I was still talking to him I went to the main screen of my phone to see whether I had missed any call from my parents by any chance but there was none. "Ok I mean it's surprising how they just made a sudden plan," was my response to it. "Forget that and talk to them later, just listen to this first; you just won't believe my father called me today and he sounded much less stubborn than before. He really liked your family and he is positive about getting us married! Vaani I just knew it, it has been eight good years since we are friends and see! No love marriage has ever happened in my family before, but somehow my persistent efforts worked, I made things happen!" Sahil went on breathlessly and happily about it, but my thoughts ceased.

I could not utter any words, where Sahil my closest friend and my support system was so elated about the new turns that the things in his family had taken I was in a shock about this sudden news and why? When I was actually expecting this to happen someday. Lost in my own new world I had gone so ahead that I completely forgot the things that I had left behind. Yes Sahil loved me and still! But for me...I was such a different person now, from being simple, work-oriented and stable I had transformed into an outgoing, materialistic and an unstable persona. I still had my friends around and I always wanted them to be around but perhaps I wanted them to play different roles in my life. Looking at Sahil's excitement and the way he sounded I had just no strength to utter any word from my mouth because I knew I had no romantic inclination towards him anymore and I had no heart to get married to him at that point. I had never seen him that happy in the last eight years and I did not have any strength to curb his happiness at that moment. Years back he had told me that he will always stay by my side but it will take some time for things in his family to work. His family was completely orthodox, he had told me of a situation where once one of his cousins was married to someone he liked after which no one in the house ever spoke to them again. He did not want this to happen to us, and so he mentioned to his family about me, gave time to everyone in the house and stayed persistent on it and here he was. I think persistent efforts and a true heart never fails. Sahil had both. "What, no response no reaction?" he said. "No, no I am just thinking how come my parents didn't even tell me before they went." "How does it matter anyway, just look how things turned!" His voice was echoing with happiness and the more it did the more my heart sank! "But then where are you planning to be in future?" I interrupted him. "See it depends upon the opportunities I get, I may try for some higher degrees now. If so I will stay around here in Lucknow itself, I may also go somewhere outside India for a while and then come back. I am not sure. Let's see how things unfold." "But you will be responsible for me as well Sahil. How can you just go ahead with the wedding without a concrete plan? My future prospects are as important as yours." "Yes of course, but then I believe this is not a moment to discuss all this, we have got something which we have been trying for from past many years, it's time to rejoice, feel happy, celebrate." "I don't think I am prepared for the wedding, Sahil," is all that I could say. "Things will still take time Vaani. Don't worry it's not just tomorrow even I need my time." "Not that man I just can't keep you happy. Please understand. It's not about time. I am a very different person altogether now, I am not the Vaani you fell in love with eight years ago." "Take your time, relax," he said. Sahil had an extremely positive outlook towards things, at times it was something that gave me the strength that I needed. But now when he was extruding positivity despite me being so open and clear. I just hated it. I had shown no interest in the wedding plan or in him but he still believed that no matter how much I change I will revert back to my true self, as per him it was just circumstantial. All this was just a temporary paint that I had over me because I was in a very different environment and with very different people.

I went back to my accommodation because I had no mood to window shop anymore. I felt disturbed and confused. I called my mother, "You people visited Sahil's house and you thought it wasn't important to tell me about it?" I questioned her "*Arre beta* it was not a planned visit. Your father had some work in the city and so we ended up meeting his family. They seemed fine, the house is average, but they are simple and yes very orthodox for sure," she said. "Did you have a word with Sahil by the way, what was his family's response about the meeting?" She asked. "Yes I just spoke to him, his father is turning positive he said, things will work out soon! But then I don't want this wedding and all mom," I guess I sounded irritated. "But you were prepared for it ever since you finished your post-graduation *beta,* what now?" "If they took so many years to agree for the wedding then it's not my fault that I changed mom, please stop this wedding drama!" Well now I was rude. My mom handled things a little more diplomatically and then she was not the one that I ever discussed my heart out with, so we stopped on a note where even she told me to take my time. Akash hadn't spoken to me in the past one week then. After I settled with the family talks and came back to myself I clearly knew why I did not want to get married. Why I had changed so much and why I was behaving the way I was. I thought over many times and finally called Akash. I wanted to tell him everything very clearly and I wanted to be straightforward and tell him that I loved him and I wanted to get married to him. I dialled his number, the phone rang, and for a second my heart started thumping a little more than usual, thinking about his response and hoping that he would be in a good mood. Akash was moody for sure and it was important to approach him for any such serious discussions at the right moment, **User Busy** is what displayed on my screen and I got a busy tone. He had disconnected my call; it wasn't his day off from work so I thought he must be busy in doing something, kept my phone aside and waited impatiently for his call. In another five minutes time I got a message, it was Akash and it read "Babe! I am outside the MDs office I am resigning from the job today and am flying to Australia tonight for some paperwork and formalities; I will be back in a week's time." "Whaaaat!" I replied. "You didn't tell me you were going so soon, when will we talk? I need to talk to you about something important." "I am not going away for good babe! Today I will be rushing because I need to take the flight; we will talk once I am back." He had told me that he will be resigning but I didn't know things will happen so soon. I badly wanted to talk to him I couldn't afford delays; I couldn't afford to face millions of questions from my parents, from Sahil and from myself. Take me and fly Akash don't leave me alone my heart cried aloud. But then hearts are unfortunate. They don't realize that they are only meant to pump blood, no one bothers when they cry.

I went and sat on the terrace amidst some silence and gazed at the sky which looked beautiful in different shades of red and orange as the dusk was setting in. I looked above at the heaven for quite some time just to see how the sky was turning darker with the setting sun and the passing time. Even my life was passing through different shades. And as I gazed above and waited for the next shade of the heaven above, all I could do at this moment was sit back and look at my own life to see the color it showed me next.

CHAPTER 25

In the situation that I was, I felt trapped, I needed to talk to someone who was neutral to all this, someone who could see things from both the angles and talk to me about it. Manav was the best person to approach and discuss. I didn't want to discuss this with him over the phone though, because direct means of communication is what I needed the most at that point in time. Fortunately, we had a long weekend coming up and I planned a trip to Bangalore where Manav joined me for a day. It was always great to visit that city. It reminded me of my post-graduation days, it reminded me how everyone motivated me to learn Kannada, and how I did. I had taken an overnight bus to the place and the moment I got down from the bus the air itself felt different and pleasant with a tinge of cold, where you don't really know if you have to put on that jacket which you are carrying or just enjoy the goosebumps that you are getting. Natives from there always complained though that their city wasn't as pleasant and as serene as it was originally because of all the migrants from different parts of the country, but for outsiders like me, it was heaven. I was putting up at one of my aunts place and I took an auto for the same, and to my surprise I wasn't able to talk Kannada that fluently anymore. Telugu was taking over and overlapping it. I smiled to myself, I felt like I was home after a really long time and had forgotten the rules of the house. Though after two broken attempts I finalized the rates and explained my destination to the auto driver. I was supposed to meet Manav only after eleven and so I went and dozed off, woke up fresh and headed for the coffee shop near my place where we had decided to meet.

I was sitting and gazing out of the window when I saw him walking towards the shop; he waved at me and smiled. Manav had very small eyes on a relatively big face and whenever he smiled or laughed they appeared even tinier, even I was happy to see him. A good friend is much more than thousands of other characters in your life I feel. He was dressed up fairly well in a checkered shirt, jeans that went well with it and loafers. No matter what the occasion was he was one of those people who believed in showing up well. "Woo! Look at someone" I smiled and received him; he smiled back and flaunted about the different places from where he had got his clothes and shoes on the previous day. After the little warm-up talks, and after we decided the order for both of us he asked me. "Ok, so what is that important thing which you wanted to discuss?" "Hmm...I am in the middle of nowhere Manav," I started. "I have no clue where my life is heading, I feel dull, I have thousands of thoughts in my head all the time." I was lost. "You seem to have lost weight actually, I did not want to mention it but you do look dull and meek," he commented, "I do right? I knew it" I said and became a little upset again. Girls forget all their worries when the worry of their skin, weight or hair takes over them. I started looking at myself and I started asking him some annoying questions like lost? How much? So I look weak? Have my cheeks also gone in? So is it significant or tolerable? And so on and so forth to which he laughed and said, "I hope I am not here to discuss that something serious," I laughed back and continued. "It's about my future, my wedding, the thing is that my parents visited Sahil's house last week without any prior notice and his father is all positive about getting us married now." "Wow so that's good right?" He was surprised about how that could be a problem. If I was taken back in time by two years, even I may have responded similarly. But unfortunately unlike how we 'undo' everything in the technical systems that we operate no matter how tech-savvy we get, we still can't 'undo' things from our life. "Good! Hmm... unfortunately no Manav I am just not the same person that I was. I can't justify this relationship anymore I feel." "You have changed for sure Vaani and I am the last person to deny that. Sometimes I too feel that I have lost that close friend of mine, but wake up! Sahil truly cares for you, he is someone who just lets you be and that's all that matters. He will never ask you to revert back," he explained. "You are not getting my point, I don't love him, Manav. He is a friend just like how you are, someone I like and I love to be with, but how can I marry him?" I continued to argue. "Don't behave like a kid Vaani, now don't tell me that you want to wait till you fall in love with someone, a good bond and understanding is the prime thing for taking your relation forward." "I am not saying I will wait till I feel love. I already love someone else, Manav." He looked at me in suspicion for a minute's time, his eyes wanted to say I already knew it, and his nose, of course, was getting a little annoyed at me. "Don't tell me," is what he said next. It was understood that he knew my feelings about Akash, and it was understood that he didn't like him at all. "Yes," I said and raised an eyebrow. "Of all people that silly boy, I told you to stay away from him." "What do you even know about him Manav? And how can you call him silly, if he is silly then what are you?" I shouted. "Look at you women, love doesn't make you be like this with your friends," he looked hurt. Yes he had been there for me whenever I needed him and he was not doing anything wrong now as well. It was his opinion and I should have asked and argued with him more about it rather than getting agitated at it. I was lucky that he still sat there with me even after I told him a hundred other rude things which I shouldn't have and he still argued on how I would be wrong if I reject Sahil's proposal. The same Manav had questioned me if I felt any "wow" feeling for Sahil two years back when we had spoken in the Ramoji film city but in the two-year span he befriended Sahil himself and was of the idea that I couldn't get a better person. He lectured me later on how understanding and friendship are the pillars of a married relation, and how the rest is just a momentary high and should not be considered important. Everyone else who knew me for long ended up supporting Sahil as well. But then I do not know why they were not seeing things from my perspective. Why were they not realizing that you can't force feelings, and why they were not letting me be the way I was. But sometimes people see what you don't, sometimes your own perspective is biased and blind and sometimes you don't learn until you actually fall.

CHAPTER 26

It had been more than two months since Akash had returned back from Australia, but was out of the city for some or the other reason and so we were neither able to meet nor talk in peace. With the uneasiness that I was facing all that I did throughout the day was, think about my good times with him, think about my life before I met him and think about what future may show me. Both my mother and Sahil had told me to take my time, but directly or indirectly they were still taking out the wedding topic and they still wanted to know what I had thought about it. Rather than being the chirpy-self, I used to spend time being quiet and aloof at my workplace also. My interaction with Shivani had certainly increased. When free, we used to sit for hours together discussing deeper things in life. It's funny how we turn more philosophical in any adverse situation and the moment the adversity goes we revert again. Unlike previously when I was occupied with my phone most of the times. Now I was avoiding talking to my own near and dear ones perhaps because I was trying to run away from the situation in which I was, because I intentionally wanted to delay things, till I settled them in my mind, till I settled them between me and Akash. I used to talk a lot about Akash to Sahil just to allay my mind but as always, I did not dare to tell him about my intimacy with him.

After a really long wait one evening Akash called me and made a plan to meet up, "Baby I am sorry to keep you waiting for so long. I have been too occupied and things are very rough at my end. You are always so sweet to me; I want to spend one full day with you somewhere in peace, just the two of us. I will discuss all that I have been up to for all these days. I will book a room for both of us tomorrow in a five star in the center of the city. Let's just unwind from our stresses." "Done!" I was more than eager to spend time with him. "Day after tomorrow then, it's a week off for you and I will keep myself totally free," he said. That day he came to my place at four in the morning, we were supposed to check in the hotel at five because he did not want to waste any time to get there. He was the "*late to sleep and later to rise*" category and every time he did such sweet little things like compromising his sleep just for me, it touched my heart. I hadn't gotten up that early in the morning for a very long time, the sky was still dark and it was quiet all over. The guard of my accommodation was awake to fill some water in the tanker on the ground floor, and a lady who worked in the accommodation mess was getting the utensils ready to cook for the day. I was surprised at how hard people work and what all people do while I still sleep. The guard smiled at me and asked me if I was going to my native to which I said a no and moved out. Akash was waiting in his car outside my place, "Good morning...Yawn!" He was half sleepy and so was I but my sleep always disappeared when I saw him. I happily sat with him and we started for the hotel which was a good fifteen kilometers from my place. "I am seeing you after the longest time ever!" I said like a typical girl who tries to act a little cute in front of the man she admires. "Hmm..." is all I got. "You won't believe, yesterday I had slept so late and still I am all fresh." "Hmm..." is what I got again. "The roads are so empty no, otherwise this half a kilometer would have taken you a good twenty minutes." "Hmm..." said the sleepy guy for the third time. "You are so quiet." "God you talk so much early in the morning at four also," he finally looked at me and smiled. We exchanged a quick kiss on that and then the little conversations from my side continued. Obviously, I wouldn't have mentioned anything serious to him at that point in time, so just the little chit-chatting happened between us early in the morning. We reached the hotel, checked in our room and both of us slept till it was time for breakfast. We went outside in one of their restaurants where they had displayed a lot of things for buffet breakfast. I had some white bread, milk, chocolate flakes and bull's eye egg, whereas he added a lot of typical south Indian breakfast to his plate including a couple of *vadas, sambhar, upma,* and three varieties of *chatnis.* He looked at my plate and I looked at his. "We are so damn different" He laughed. "What have you been up to man? I missed you so much," it was a little moment of awe for both of us. "Aah! What do I say? I don't know what's going on? I had been to Australia and because of some paperwork and formalities there it will take some more time till I can go and start working with them. I have resigned from here already, I feel like I am in the middle of nowhere." "That's ok, Akash. You have been working very hard for the past so many years, a little time off shouldn't bother you that much. You have something in hand already so sooner or later things will fall in place," I assured him. "Those guys have told me it may take a couple of months, I think I resigned in a hurry. Now all that I am doing is freelancing! Be it here or out of the city most of the times." He told me many such small things about his professional life, and how it was difficult for him now without a routine schedule and routine salary. It was definitely a difficult phase for him as well. We were sailing in an almost similar boat which was passing through a patch of turbulent waters, just that my turbulence comprised of personal and his of the professional dimension of life. He told me about many other small little problems that he was facing and how he was trying to cope up with everything.

I tried to start a conversation about how things were at my end but he said he rather wanted to unwind and relax for a while before we discussed anything serious again. Even I took a break and just chilled and lazed in the room with him. It was time for lunch, we played some good music on the television and ordered food in the room itself. I wasn't hungry and chose not to eat anything. "You are the sweetest," he started. "I feel so good with you, I really like your company," he was starting to get a little closer to me, though I was a little more away this time because of the millions of things which were running on my mind. But then when it was Akash I had to give up to him always. While we were completely engrossed in each other the doorbell rang, we laughed and he opened the door. Our lunch was ready and was served in the room itself. He quickly arranged it at the table and asked me to join. "No somehow I don't want to." "Even if you are not hungry you have to," he forced me. I joined him and picked up a little piece of chapatti and started to play with it. "What is this way of eating?" He got annoyed and mixed some rice, curd, and spices on the spoon and fed it to me with his hand. "I have never done this to anyone," he said. I felt happy; I knew I was with the right man.

Later that evening he finally asked me, "So what did you want to discuss?" His mood was good, he was lightened up a little from his personal turmoil after the time we spent together and so I knew that it was the right time to initiate the serious talks. "Akash, just like you even I am going through a little rough patch in my personal life," while I spoke to him he continued to look at the television to which I stared at him for a moment to make sure that he listens. "Go ahead I am listening," he said. "See my parents spoke to one of my friend's family without telling me even once and want us to get married. Sahil, remember I had mentioned him." I was expecting a surprised look from him, or I was at least expecting that he will switch off the television and be a little more attentive. But to my own surprise he gave me a casual look and said, "Good for you, go ahead," and continued to munch some chips and stared at the television. I had gathered all my strength to say that and this was the least that I expected from the man I was crazy about. I was shocked at his reaction. Did I hurt him? I thought. But then this was something I had to discuss with him and so I gathered some words and spoke again, "Go ahead! How? I don't want to Akash, you know I like you." "What are you talking? Don't irritate me!" He made an angry face, took out a cigarette and started smoking. "See, I am already going through a lot ok, don't add to it by behaving like this. You are a very good friend and by behaving like this don't lose your position in my life." I was almost in tears but he continued to get angry. "I don't have any intentions to add to your troubles Akash. I rather want to be a part of it. I am not in any hurry, let things settle. I am always there and I am always the same. I just want to tell you that I do want to marry you." It took a lot of effort from me to say that. I had never expressed that much to anyone. I had poured out completely on what I felt for him. I couldn't afford to wait for a step from his side. I had to be clear because we were already very far in our relation. He took his cigarette which was half burnt by then, left it in the ashtray and got up, "I can't marry you! Did I ever say that we will or did I make some promises? You were always better off as just a very good friend that's all. Even you know that. So go ahead he is a nice guy, be happy and let me be happy." "But we are so close Akash. What is the reason...I mean..." I couldn't gather words, "Close! Did I force you to be close? Don't get that in between ok!" He stared at me in anger and then cooled down a bit and said, "You are very nice no doubt, but then see I never thought about you in such a way. You were always better off only as a very good friend. Please get that and so let's just stop this discussion." I was almost beginning to classify friends in my head now, 'a very close friend with benefits and with an added advantage of being your punching bag anytime' is where I thought I was fitting. It was eight in the evening already and I had to join work from the next day. After the outburst amongst both of us, there was no point staying back in the hotel until the next day morning. He said he had something to attend at home and so we had to push out. He went down at the reception to clear the bills and other formalities, while I sat in the room in some hollowness for another five minutes before I started to wrap up things. In a fraction of second while I was glancing through the place to see if I had left anything in the room my eyes caught Akash's half burnt cigarette which lay in the ashtray. I don't know why but I took it and kept it safe in my wallet.

CHAPTER 27

Till the day I met Akash my confusions were totally different. While after I met him things changed completely for me again. The pointer for my questions which was previously on my parents for their accidental visit, and on Sahil for still being so positive was now on Akash. But coincidentally even though my pointer was at him it was just stuck there thinking what to ask. I liked him and he never forced me for anything, he did take the first steps but I always had things in my hand, I always had a choice to step back. But probably my updates on love and romance were totally old school; my idea of romance was like how we read in the fairy tales where the prince charming kissed the princess and never said you are my friend. He rather said he loved her, or like how they featured in the old Indian movies where if the actor and the actress sang a song or held hands it meant they were in love they never turned out to be just friends later. The modern romance was different, the modern friends were different and perhaps the modern wedding was different too! Always being engrossed in my books and work during my student days, the idiotic me never updated my basic concepts on love and friendship, had

I done that I would have never felt unsaid things and I wouldn't have misunderstood this modern day friendship for love. I was never an advocator of these changes in basic emotional concepts which had happened in today's time but now I was finding myself stuck and entangled in it. It's hard to learn new concepts though. So my mind was still not giving up on Akash, it kept on defending him, it kept on saying that no matter how much things change this isn't just friendship he loves me for sure. Maybe he didn't know how to react, maybe he wasn't able to express directly in front of me, yes it was possible I thought and in another moment of bewilderment I ended up messaging him, "Hey! Hope all is good at your end?" I didn't want to write anything more than that till he replied. I was always of the thought that people who are not that expressive otherwise are freer to express in messages. He replied a little late, "All good, have been busy with some work." "Hmm...why can't you marry me?" I am surprised at how straight I was, but probably a broken heart and a bewildered mind doesn't think anything before it talks. "I can't, don't ask me that stupid question again and again and irritate me." "Sorry, please don't get angry. This is just to ask you if it is because of anything which went wrong from my side," I typed while tears rolled down my eyes and I blinked more and constantly. "I never said anything or did anything which I did not say at all. You know about me since day one. I never thought about you in such a way. Why are you acting so weird all of a sudden?" "Yes true, sorry my bad. It's some emotional outburst I guess, maybe I am missing home or something." Tears continued to roll down constantly after that. I felt some strange discomfort inside me as if my soul wanted to separate from my body. As if I wanted to leave everything and just run. But where could I have gone?

Akash and I did not speak for quite a few days after that. I did not know what to talk whereas he was occupied with his work. Questions from my family had multiplied because they were oblivious to my state of mind. The only problem that they had was about keeping a check on the auspicious dates and the wedding halls. I used to hear everything with a light mind and tried to focus more on my work which kept me occupied for most of the time during the day. I bought some books which kept me occupied for the time after work. I needed books, and they turned out to be my best support then, television always showed some or the other romance, or song which reminded me of Akash so I barely used to switch it on. Even the movie theatres reminded me of him and so now I was no more enjoying watching films unlike previously. I used to feel tied up and I didn't know if things would ever be back to what they were. I didn't know if I would ever be back to how I was; happy, content and free of the millions of things in my head.

Festival of colors, *Holi* was approaching a couple of weeks later and so I planned a trip home. Every time I took a flight from one place to the other I used to observe the change in crowd, language, and peoples' attitude when I stood at the conveyor belt to wait for my luggage and appreciate the diversity that existed in our own country. The moment I exited out on the Lucknow airport I was immediately surrounded by too many cab and auto drivers. There was a lot of rush and noise around and so I struggled to figure out where my family driver was, walked fast and got into the car. While on my way back home he asked me small little things like how it was to work so far from home, about the weather and food in Hyderabad etc. On my way, I could see some vendors selling colors and fancy water guns for the festival and some sweet shops which had made an extension way ahead of their shop to attract customers for the variety of things that they had. All this looked very festive but somehow this festival never fascinated me. On the contrary, I was always scared of colors maybe because I never tried exposing myself to it and the fear just multiplied over the years. Where the entire city was painted green, blue and red I used to still stay indoors and read something or watch television till the afternoon when everybody came back and it was then that the festival actually began for me. For me it was all about cooking a different meal, eating together with the family and meeting people in the evening. This time as expected there had to be some serious discussions about my wedding as well. On the Holi evening after we finished our respective works, my parents sat with me and started off, "We wished Sahil's family for new years and Holi from our side, they sounded happy and his father said he wanted the two of you to get married in the next auspicious time which will follow immediately in the coming month. Their family has certain firm believes in choosing the dates only on certain days and so we have left it to them to decide upon that. How about you and Sahil? Both of you wanted some time and we already pushed things by eight months now." Asked my mother. I was literally pitying myself hearing all this, ever since I was young the one thing which I was always excited about was my big day, my wedding and now that things were actually happening and progressing I was in a stupid state of mind. It wasn't about Sahil. He was one of the most eligible bachelors that could have been, it wasn't about me needing more time with him either I knew him well for a good eight years then. It was just about me and how I changed things for myself. "What should I say mom, why can't we push the things a little more; I am still thinking because it'll be such a big change for me. I will have to leave the world that I have created for myself in Hyderabad and come back and start fresh." "But someday it has to be started fresh! You are a girl and you can't live independently throughout your life. You know the boy well and he is doing just fine. I don't see any hitch anywhere. Then even Sahil has been too positive at his place and they are already planning on the dates, weddings aren't pushed like this for small little reasons," she tried explaining to me. I think the biggest reason to push a wedding date was that the girl was still not in a positive frame of mind for it. But then logically speaking there was no hitch, both the boy and the girls age was advancing, the families were ready, the auspicious dates were nearing and the decision had to be made before the so-called wedding halls were booked. Woo! Sometimes being logical is the worst that we can do. Succumb to the circumstances and the fact that I had no reason to deny, because the guy in my head had no intentions to be with me at all, and the guy who wanted to marry me wanted to be with me despite anything that came his way I gave up for the wedding!

Sahil was in the same city, I met him on the day when I was leaving back to Hyderabad after my *Holi* leaves. The plan was to meet him and then be dropped by him to the airport. I was meeting him after one good year or so. He was too happy to see me and he was excited to show me around the place where he worked. I wore my casual jeans with a plain white t-shirt and carried my luggage with me as well. With Sahil I never had to think of what I was wearing or how I was looking because it never mattered to him. He liked me the way I was. We went to his room to keep my luggage, he held my hand and smiled. "Finally, Vaani," is all that he said and he was getting emotional. "Hmm yes," I smiled half-heartedly to that and withdrew my hand. "Take your time," he said again and we went out to have coffee and snacks. He spoke about things that his parents and siblings were discussing regarding the wedding, his work, his possible future plans and so on and so forth. My mind and heart were floating in some other world I was attentive and inattentive both. But I certainly felt good; his positivity reduced my anxiety and made me happier. After a couple of hours, he dropped me to the airport and we said our goodbyes. I plugged my earphones and kept my documents ready to enter the inside of the airport. After finishing the formalities as I sat in the waiting area in front of the boarding gate tears welled up in my eyes. This time it was not because of Akash. This time it was because of me and my helplessness. I just wished that I was able to give a little of the same affection back to Sahil as much as he had for me. My thoughts were broken with the boarding announcement and I departed from Lucknow to say a final goodbye to Hyderabad, my second home.

CHAPTER 28

My wedding was finalized, and the dates were announced to all the near and dear ones. It was scheduled in the immediate next month after I came back from home. I was told that it was some auspicious time for weddings. Like in every workplace even we had a notice period for which I was required to serve the organization before I finally left. For us, it was a good three months. I gave my resignation so that I could start my notice period soon because now that Sahil was not here I had to move. We had some discussions about him moving to Hyderabad city but he did not show any interest and was very clear that he would not want to relocate even if he gets the best of opportunity. "But then I will have to start it all fresh in Lucknow, I don't know if things will work for me," considering that I was always a work-oriented person I had shown that concern. "Things don't happen overnight Vaani, and then you are very talented, work for it and I am sure you will create opportunities for yourself," he had assured me. Of course, Sahil was the one who had kept me motivated over a period of years, he was the one who had made me pursue my post-graduation and he was the one who always kept me positive. Thus, I agreed to what he said and hoped for the best. Resigning a job always shows us some mixed emotions I guess, a part of us which is tired of our routine, irritated by the internal politics and bugged with the HR wants to dance out of joy whereas the other part of us which gets attached to the place and the people feels sad. It was surprising that the moment I said I will be leaving in the next three months, everyone around me changed. People started opening up to me more, going out with me more and were much more kind and considerate towards me, unlike the days when I was working in a routine.

My heart was still heavy and I was in no mood to socialize but I had to be practical. I was getting married and I had to live up to it and then there were so many people who were showering love and care on me. I couldn't afford to let their affection go in vain. Yes there were some quiet times when I had an outburst of tears and the rather heavy emotions overtook the lighter ones, when Akash just failed to leave my thoughts. But at such times I used to just sit up on my accommodation terrace for few minutes or a couple of hours, write something in my personal folder, feel better and get back to reality. In a short span, we had to finalize a lot of things for the wedding. I had made a checklist and every day after the hospital hours I used to get busy in some or the other work to tick one thing off at a time. Here is a glimpse of how my list looked like;

- *Finalize the wedding dress and jewellery,*
- *High heels to wear underneath,*
- *Something to wear for the rituals after the reception* is *over,*
- *Match separate jewellery for the post-reception part as well,*
- *Get wedding invites printed for friends and so and so forth.*

There were five proper dresses on my list for separate occasions besides the main reception! No wonder Indian weddings are a huge affair I thought. I had decided to get fifty invites printed separately for my friends which were supposed to be other than the ones which my parents were getting done. On one of my day off I went out to get that work done, people had suggested me *Gowliguda* location in old Hyderabad. I started my day early that day, considering the heavy traffic on the way it took me the usual two hours to reach there. The place was flooded with little shops which sold wedding cards, and it was flooded with people like me who came to shop for the invites, there were some parents with their daughter or son, some boys in a group of friends, and some lone people like me. Everyone had different specifications and choices. There were huge varieties of invites which I saw, they had ones for separate religions as well, and some invites came with a box of dry fruits which looked fancy but costed a fortune. I chose simple roll on cards which were big enough to print an invitation message, my idea was to give that little notice like thing in a fancy bottle or tied to a chocolate box etc. I bought fifty of them got them printed and then tied them with ribbons on boxes or kept them in the bottles. This fitted well with my budget and looked much fancier than the ones which the vendors had shown me.

The day was nearing and I had to leave Hyderabad once again for a month to finish my wedding; a week before I finally flew for the big day I started distributing the invites, I visited the MD of my organization first, then the HR and then my colleagues. "Wow it's such an amazing invite," said someone. "So sweet," said someone else. "I wish I could come Vaani," was Shivani's reaction. She gave me a small present as a mark of remembrance from her side as well. "Did you invite Dr. Akash?" She asked me. "Not yet," was my blunt reply. "What was his reaction to know that you are getting married?" "Nothing madam he was happy for me," I said. Somehow maybe she figured that she had touched the wrong cords to which she tried to console me and assure me simultaneously and said, "See Sahil has been your friend and he is a very nice guy I feel. You have taken the best decision. May God keep you both happy always." I thanked her for her care and affection and got lost in my own thoughts after that. I was not able to decide if I should invite Akash. Ever since our last chat we were lesser in touch with each other. I messaged him only on and off to which he replied after hours or days together saying that he was busy. Akash was someone with whom I had shared a lot of my things, and he was also someone whom I trusted a lot. I never wanted this bond between us to change. Yes things hadn't worked well between us for the past couple of days, and things were not like how I wanted them to be, but did that mean losing a very close friend as well I wondered. But simultaneously I didn't want him to come for my wedding that was for sure and that was obvious. It's funny how we complicate things and relations right? I was sure that I loved Akash, and I was still not able to let him go. I knew that any attachment to him was keeping me bound and unfocused but somehow I was still trying to hold on to it. Unaware of any further complications that the future may have brought I still wanted to be friends with him. Anyways, I thought quite a lot and decided to give him a call and accordingly decide what needed to be done. Luckily he did answer my call, he sounded a little dull than his usual self. "Ya tell me," he said. The thing with friends and people with whom you bond too well is that no matter after how many days you speak to them the 'hello' immediately after answering the call disappears. They always answer the call by anything other than the usual "Hello!" "Hey how have you been, I was just thinking that we should catch up someday this week." "I am too busy, will see sometime next month," he said. "But I won't be here next month, Akash. I am going home for a month and there is a lot that I need to tell you." "Today evening by around seven then, come down to my place. I haven't been too well so I don't want to go out." "Sure," I said as usual. For Akash I could cancel all my prior plans, for Akash I never ever thought even once if I was occupied with anything else, for Akash it was always a yes of course immediately.

I went back home early from work and quickly took out an invite with the biggest chocolate box for him and his family. Since I was going for a formal meeting, I wore a yellow *salwar kameez* and simple heels, I kept the invite in my handbag, checked for my wallet and phone, booked a cab and pushed out. Throughout the time that I traveled from my place to his all that I was thinking was about the things that I needed to tell him and how. After all the awkwardness that had happened between us in the hotel, we were still comfortable with each other, and maybe he would react as casually I thought as he did when I had first told him that my parents were on a lookout and wanted me to get married. But in either case I was still on the other side of the story and I was tensed. I called him as soon as I reached his place. "Come inside, the door is open," he said. I walked in, he stood at the door to receive me, didn't smile as much as his usual self. "Come" is all he said and went and sat inside on one of the sofas in the living room. He stood there staring at his phone and I sat there looking around. I couldn't see anyone else in the house. "So what happened?" he asked me. "Where is your mom?" I asked. "Everyone else went to Coorg for a vacation, they will be back only after five days." "Oh ok, so how are you managing your meals?"

"Sometimes out, sometimes some friend comes and gives, it's manageable," he said. We spoke about random things for a while. And then I finally broke my silence on the wedding. "My wedding is next month, Akash. I was in two minds ever since I spoke to you about it last, but then I had to give up," while I said this I was looking away and not straight into his eyes because I felt more comfortable that way. But within a fraction of second as I said that he looked straight at me without even blinking once. I felt awkward and I felt a strange sensation of goosebumps all over my body. Because I felt love in that glance but the moment I looked at him he said, "Congratulations" and looked away. I spoke about how the wedding was more like a duty to fulfill, how we needed to understand our responsibilities after we get married and so on and so forth. To all that I said he didn't give much reaction except, "Hmm right" or "true" in between. We barely caught each other's glance. It looked as if we were rather trying to avoid looking at each other. After an hour since we spoke, he told me that he had to attend a party and will have to leave in some time from then. I got up to go to which even he stood up called me near him and gave me a big bear hug which lasted somewhere in minutes, as if he was just trying to feel my warmth for one last time before I left for my wedding. He continued to hold me, wrapped my face in his hands and kissed me on my forehead. I had tears in my eyes and both of us did not need any words to describe our feelings. It was as if we both knew what was left unsaid, as if we both were reading the silence between us. "Keep him happy and stay happy, if so I will also be happy," he said and we parted. Neither did I give him any verbal or printed invite nor did he ask for one. Neither did I want him to attend the event nor did he want to come I guess. I went back to my accommodation and stared at my wedding things spread all over. There was some jewellery that I needed to sort and some invites that I needed to wrap. I just kept everything aside. I didn't want to sort or do anything at that point of time, all that I did was opened my laptop and wrote some thousand odd words in my personal folder again.

CHAPTER 29

"Is your dance for the *sangeet* ready?" asked my mother who was all excited about the wedding. I had reached back home and everyone around me was ready for the event. The house was completely festive; a lady was called to give me a head massage every day. Woo! I thought, if weddings were all about this then I wish we get married every year. Everyone in the family was concerned about my diet, and my skin. I asked them how did it matter because I felt you are what you are and why should you be so concerned about how you look on the day of wedding. To which they explained to me that all the events are captured in an album and at the end of the day you want yourself to look good in the frame. I didn't know if Sahil's family was preparing him similar to how I was being prepared. "Hmm...dance, I will do it mom," I said. "But it's a big event, we are hosting a lot of people on that day and you will have an individual performance which all the guests will be looking forward to." "Chill mom I will manage," I had told her. North Indian weddings begin at least five days prior to the main reception in every house I guess. At least in my house it did. From some rituals to sangeet, to Mehendi, many such small events were lined up for me. And if you are from a relatively smaller place and not a metropolitan city then every person around is more or less related to you and so you need to be extra conscious in dressing or dancing. My entire room was flooded with my own suitcases and boxes, the first thing which I did after I reached back to my place was sorting those things and putting them in a separate closet which made me feel a little more organized and a little less panicky.

I was finally getting married, and now there was no turning back. In the midst of all the noises and chaos that existed in my house Akash still kept visiting my mind. The moment everyone around left me alone for some time all that troubled me was that kiss on the forehead, all that I was confused about was whether I had even told him properly that I loved him and I wanted to marry him. I just wanted to be assured that he was never inclined towards me; he never wanted to marry me. I called Manav. "Hey bride to be, I was just booking my tickets to come to your place, how are things going?" "That's great Manav. I am glad you will meet everyone at my place. And more than that I am happy that you will be there; everything is going fine. I was trying to prepare for my solo dance performance tomorrow evening," I said. "Wow! Now I do need a video recording for that, mind you." He demanded, "Of course you will get it, buddy! Manav something is just eating me up. I still feel that Akash loved me. He just pretends, for what I also don't know, I am not sure if I approached him properly. I am not sure why he said we were just friends," I was sobbing again. "Vaani either stop this nonsense or never talk to me ever again," he said. Manav never tolerated anything beyond a point. He got too angry at me. But I am so surprised how everything just failed to affect me. It was like I got some *Akash attack* every now and then and all that I needed was the right conversation, something that could calm me and take me out of it, I tried writing but it didn't help. I remembered he messaged me clearly that he wasn't inclined towards me romantically. I went back to my Whatsapp chat history searched for the exact conversation, took a screenshot of it and read it to feel better:

Me: Hmm...why can't you marry me?

Akash: I can't, don't ask me that stupid question again and again & irritate me

Me: Sorry. Please don't get angry. This is just to ask you if it is because of anything which went wrong from my side

Akash: I never said anything or did anything which I did not say at all. You know about me since day one. I never thought about you in such a way. Why are you acting so weird all of a sudden?

Me: Yes true, sorry my bad, it's some emotional outburst I guess, maybe I am missing home or something

Yes, he had made it clear that he never wanted to marry me. It did allay me but I recalled every second that we had spent together over and over again to know where and what went wrong. Not able to find any reason I always ended up blaming my blunt nose and my big teeth. But whatever it was he had been too clear and I should stop behaving like this I thought and got busy in preparing my dance for the next day evening. All that I didn't know at that point in time was that I would be staying with those thoughts, and read those messages for n more times for many years to come!

Two days prior to the wedding some of my close friends including Manav came and made me feel alive. Because of them my panic levels came down. It is surprising how we feel both excitement and panic simultaneously during our wedding. I was excited about everyone coming from so far just for me, and about the whole dressing up and showing up thing. Whereas the panic came because I was about to enter a new phase and explore a new dimension of my life, where I didn't know what to expect. On the day of marriage, we shifted to the venue where the lawn and the rooms were booked in advance. The decorations started since the morning. In fact, some part was done one day prior already. I observed the immense preparations and manpower that was put up just for one event which didn't even last for a complete twenty-four hours. I had suggested my parents to keep it as a smaller affair. After all, the wedding was all about rituals for two people to tie a knot but then they argued that they always wished it the big way and so I just left it to them. What I had done from my side though was that, I contacted an NGO to take food from the wedding and distribute it to the needy. At least leftover food is something that I didn't want and so both me and Sahil had decided to proceed for the cause. I was chirpy and smiley for all the events and throughout the wedding which was more like how a child feels on the day of his annual function when he has to perform in front of everyone. I was dressed up in a heavy dress for the wedding reception and waited inside my room for things and people from the boy's side to settle after which I was told that I will have to go for the garland exchange. People were eating; talking and having a good time outside, my family members were busy with little works and running here and there whereas I sat all alone inside my room all anxious about what must be happening outside, and what will happen next. Thankfully my friends came and sat with me for some time which made me feel less tensed in the otherwise heavy dress. The garland exchange was followed by some endless pictures where all relatives, friends, family friends and other guests posed with us and we kept on smiling endlessly till our cheeks gave up. Like in any other typical wedding in the north of India there was loud music and a DJ played music simultaneously. Even we couldn't control ourselves and made sure we danced on one or two songs after the picture session was over for us. The main rituals were scheduled for in the middle of the night and had to be continued till dawn. I changed from my heavy wedding *lehenga* into a traditional saree and sat for the prayers and ritual. Even Sahil changed into something lighter for the night. I remember when I used to see people getting married, I always listened to whatever the priest said very carefully. I used to think it was an amazing feeling to listen to the things he said and feel connected to the person you were getting married to, but a little because I was tired and a little because I was anxious I couldn't be as attentive as I expected myself to be. Sahil was very attentive throughout, he sat with his back straight and with a serious face, whereas I was looking around, smiling at people and trying to keep myself awake. It was almost five in the morning when everything got over. I went inside my room and in that tired and exhausted state I got a chance to have a glance of myself in the mirror. It looked like some new me, with vermilion on my forehead and nuptial around my neck. For a moment I was shocked and turned away from my own reflection. But turning away could not change the reality. I was tied to Sahil for life and yes I had to accept that.

After some rest and breakfast I parted with everyone to leave for Sahil's native. There was no crying and consoling like after usual weddings, my family sent me with moments of laughter while I went with a new excitement as well. It was a four-hour journey that we had to cover. Sahil and I sat on the back seat of one of the cars and were left alone for the journey. I was excited to see what his place looked like and how rituals there would be like. Everything still seemed like an event, like an annual function going on, as if I was going to be back to my normal routine in Hyderabad after this. Of course, to finish my notice period I was going back but later this was going to be my new life. Sahil tried making small conversations on the way, but both of us were yawning endlessly because of the sleep deprivation that we had, we dosed and woke up only when the driver warned us that we were about to enter the village premises. I adjusted my saree, wiped the smudged kohl and tried looking livelier to prepare myself to get down.

It's strange how a girl has to keep changing her identity at different points of time, she has to move out quite a bit if not completely out of the self that she created for herself since her childhood till her wedding. And the subtle changes after she is married continue till she survives.

CHAPTER 30

In Sahil's house all auspicious functions and festivals were celebrated in his native village and thus all the rituals for us were scheduled there. Everyone in his extended family had their independent houses in and around the place and they all gathered together for any such occasion there. Any newlywed bride had to visit the village first to follow some rituals. As I was adjusting my make-up and jewellery Sahil asked me to take a veil on my head low enough to hide my face. What! But why? How will I even look around in that case? I asked, to which he told me that since people were still not as advanced there as in cities the natives of the village still expected the newlywed to be in a veil. I had to get out of the car and walk through some baskets to reach the entrance of the house, since I was wearing my wedding heels and I couldn't see anything ahead it was a little challenging for me. Some people whom I didn't see supported me from both sides and somehow I reached the main door of the house. After that I was told to sit with Sahil and a priest for some ritual. I was asked to put some rice, some water, and some other things on God's idol and on other auspicious things. I was blindly following what I was told because I still had a full veil over my face. A part of me was constantly questioning the point of praying like this when I was neither understanding nor seeing what I was doing, but then I knew that even if I tried questioning someone around they wouldn't listen. So I just quietly followed what I was told. We all tend to picture something for ourselves till we get married. I had pictured myself to be a happy bride who would love to look around, who would love to tell about herself and socialize with all new people. But here I was told to be quiet and tell anything only if asked. After the outsiders left the place I was told to sit in one of the rooms. I sat and felt a little better and I immediately put my veil up to breathe and to see where I was. My mother in law who may have noticed me came running and put my veil back, but people from outside have already left, I told her. "No no Sahil's father and other elder men of the house are there, you are always supposed to keep this in front of them," I was told. For a moment I felt suffocated. In which century are they taking me, I thought. The annual function feeling suddenly dissolved and I felt tied up. I was served some food which I had with some other married women. I couldn't look up and could barely even see what I was eating, sitting in a corner on the floor with everyone else I couldn't even swallow what I was eating because of some heavy lump which I felt in my throat. I gave up on questioning and started following whatever I was told just the way they wanted me to follow it, blindly! Someone accompanied me to my room a couple of hours later. In those few moments when I was all alone, I couldn't stop my tears. I lied down while still in some heavy saree and jewellery and since I hadn't slept well in past two days I did not realize when I dozed off.

Later that evening I was told to change my saree, be ready and sit again when women from all over the village came lifted my veil one by one and saw what I looked like. There was so much I thought that prevails in our country which makes girls insecure about their looks. None of the people staying here would have ever read the newspaper articles that are published on women's equality or seen the debates that are aired on it, though there is so much that goes on about these social issues the main target audience for it still remains oblivious to it. This was the scenario in just one village. There must be so many more, I thought, where obsolete things may still be going on in the name of culture. With so many people around I couldn't have gotten up and said anything loudly because I was a newlywed and I didn't want Sahil's family to suffer because of me. Later, of course, I conveyed many things from my side to his family members but unfortunately, it had the least of effects. I tried talking to Sahil's father but I was taken back and wasn't allowed to talk to the elder men in the house. There was certainly a huge quotient of miscommunication which existed. But despite their orthodox nature they certainly tried to take the best of care which helped me survive through the change.

Sahil was not around me for most of the part during the day. I saw him only sometime in the evening when I was sent back to my room. "Where have you been?" I asked him. "Home no, there are so many people who wanted to talk to me, some are asking about the wedding, then I went to meet one of my uncles outside, and then yes madam I am not supposed to stay around you that much," he smiled. "But I am here only because you assured me for everything Sahil. How could you just go missing without even thinking what all I must be going through?" My voice was beginning to shiver. "Oho! Don't worry I will tell my sisters and sister-in-law to stay around and take care of everything you need," he assured me. I wanted him and not people whom I didn't know that well, who I knew would not understand my point of view. But he said he was helpless and so I could do nothing but stay the way I was kept.

Finally, it was time for us to sleep. I was told that I will have to get up early in the morning at four the next day for some rituals. So I quickly changed and was ready to doze off. Sahil came and sat with me. I wanted to cry, I wanted to tell him that I was feeling out of place and different, I wanted to tell him that I was missing home, but surprisingly I didn't see the same old Sahil my best buddy in him anymore. He looked and sounded like a different man at that point in time. I wasn't able to derive the same comfort and peace from him as before. I wanted to talk to some friend at this point who I was just not able to see in him anymore. It was midnight though and none of my friends answered my call. “Relax, you will be just fine.” Sahil said and came near me. It was our first night together that day. I don’t know what all he must have thought about that night, and I don’t remember what I had pictured it to be like. All I did in that moment of emptiness was turn my face away. He turned off the lights, held me tight and said, “So Mrs. Vaani, my wait is over, finally we are together for good.” “Hmm,” I said, looked away, and submitted myself to him. While he kissed me on my neck, I continued to look away and couldn’t stop my tears from rolling down. Little did he realize how I was feeling at that point of time so all I could do was wait for him to sleep, after which I curled up in a corner of the bed and sobbed till I too slept at some point.

CHAPTER 31

After spending ten days with Sahil in his house I had to leave to Hyderabad again to finish my final notice period of two months in the city. Everyone in the house wanted me to be back soon. "What notice? Why do you even have to go back?" "Tell them to leave you within a month," etc. were the things which people at both his and my place had said to me. Even I was in no mood to join back work after my long leave but then somewhere deep down in my heart, I was happy to live my routine life for at least two months, till I acclimatized the immediate change that had happened in my life. There was a strange and comfortable smile that I had on my face the moment I landed in Hyderabad city and the moment the winds there touched my face. I forgot everything that happened in the last one month. It was as if I was back to my second home for good.

"Wow Vaani you look a little different in that attire." "Hey you have put on weight in the last one month," were people's comments. I smiled and said "Is it?" as a routine every time someone told me anything like that. "Vaani I had so many problems without you. Don't go dear, I can't believe you won't be working with us anymore after two months," poor Shivani. She was too attached to me and of course the same was my status, but we both knew that we had to move on with our respective destinies. "But anyways how did it go, I saw the pictures that you sent me, you looked so pretty in your bridal dress, just like a doll." She held me with love and said. I narrated to her all the things that happened, about the little cultural differences we have, about how my make-up took four hours all together etc. She listened to everything wholeheartedly and with enthusiasm. For next two-three days I continued to narrate the same wedding story to someone or the other after which the routine was back, somehow I was under a little more pressure than the previous days. Immediately after I came back from my wedding, the HR had started to call me a little more frequently, and expected more from me than the usual. It kept me occupied but annoyed me as well because the pressure was unnecessary and rather than congratulating me even once all that they did after I was back was dump me with all the backlogs from past one month. Even Sahil had become busy in his own routine. His hospital was busier and his workload was more. We used to talk on and off about small things almost every day. Besides just him and my friends I was now instructed to be in regular touch with all my in-laws, unlike how it was in my house where we used to either message or speak once in a while people at his side expected me to call them once every week. For a while I thought it was a little cumbersome because I did not know what to talk to all new people with whom I couldn't even share my heart out. But then later I started calling everyone more like a duty. The one thing which I was asked by everyone, each time that I spoke with them was, "When will you be back?"

I had made it a routine to go out somewhere or the other every day after work because I had very less time left to be with people of the city and to be in the city. Once during one such evening when I was going for a routine dinner with my friends my message buzzed, "Hey Mrs. Sahil! Looking good in your display picture! How have you been?" My heart started beating a little faster; it was Akash! I hadn't seen him ever since I had come back. He had called me a day prior to my wedding to congratulate me and tell me that I was the best and I shouldn't change after my marriage. After all the bitterness and silence that had happened between us I had felt too good to hear to that from him. I knew he was a friend that I never wanted to let go off. My heart wanted to contact him ever since I was back but my mind said don't meet him you still like him a lot. But now that he had contacted me himself I didn't know what to reply. I kept my phone in my hand and stared at it for ten good minutes thinking what to write. "Vaani this is wrong staring at your phone when you are with us is just not done," said one of my friend with whom I was going out for dinner. "Yes ok I apologize," I said and kept the phone in my bag. We went out to a place with live music and some energetic crowd. While everyone around was engrossed in hooting for the singer, dancing and enjoying the music, I was only physically present there, and my mind was still thinking about the reply. I was thinking whether he would still be in the city or would have left for Australia. But I tried to keep my thoughts diverted and tried to give my maximum to the people that I was with. We went out for ice cream past midnight in a popular ice cream store later, it was fun to see how the roads were still as lively as at eight in the evening, not as crowded though. We enjoyed the drive with the windows rolled down and some old classics that we played in the car, and at almost two in the night my friends dropped me back.

As soon as I came back all to myself I opened his message again and this time without even thinking twice I typed "hey all good! Came back to the city some days back, joined back work, and now I am just counting days to leave for good." I put my alarm because I had to go to work the next day and kept my phone aside, it was too late at night to expect a reply from him, the moment I turned off the lights to sleep though I saw some light on my phone, Akash had replied, "wow you are back! I have been out of town for something that I needed to attend will be back next month; I will make sure we meet before you leave."

CHAPTER 32

Time flew and the final goodbyes finally began for me. I had started giving my responsibilities to others in the hospital and all that I did was spent some quality time with all the staff and helped them if they needed any suggestions. I booked my departure tickets and the day I did, coincidentally, even Akash messaged that he was back and we scheduled a dinner on one of the rooftop restaurants near his house which was our common hang out. I didn't know when I would see him next after this and I didn't know what we were going to even talk about. I reached well ahead of time and waited for him in my white top and blue jeans. I ordered some fruit punch for myself and constantly kept switching on the front camera to see how I was looking. "*Offooo* married woman" he came from behind, patted on my head and smiled. He looked tired yet full of energy. "I did a lot of work and came, I have just no time nowadays. A lot is going on. I am leaving for Australia next week, immediately after you leave. We are leaving the city together," he was continuing almost breathlessly. "Get me a beer, my usual," he told the waiter and immediately turned to me again. "You will surely be missed. I always had such a good time with you. Don't go woman! Stay back here itself," I just stared at him both in ecstasy and agony. My mouth was shut and I had no words. "See I got my tickets also," he gave me his phone to show me his e-ticket like a small kid who has achieved something and is eager to show it to everyone around. "You will always do very well, Akash. You work very hard and I want you to get whatever you have ever dreamt off," my eyes welled up. He held my hand, "You will surely be missed," he said again. I felt like I was in a separate world... as if I had forgotten who I am and I had nothing to do or see after this. "I may marry sometime soon, there is a proposal for me, the same girl whose picture I had shown you once, we have been talking for quite some time now. She says she really likes me. I am sure she will keep me happy," He said. I was sitting in low energy till then but the moment he said this I immediately came a little ahead. "What!" I was loud. "As if I never liked you, what was our bond then? Just because I was never that expressive doesn't mean you never knew what I felt about you." I was married and I had no stepping back, I shouldn't have said what I said at that point to him, but there was a lot that was unsaid between us. A lot which had been eating me up. So perhaps I just wanted to have it clear in my mind and heart for one last time. If he would have been rude, if he would have shouted and told me not to irritate him with all this like he had told me previously, I still would have been fine I guess, but what he said was worse. What he said is something I wish he never said. "Vaani, you have no idea how much you mean to me," he was looking straight at me and had kept his phone and beer aside. "No matter what happens no one can ever take your position in my life. I feel so connected with you. I don't know what my bond with you is. I gel with you so damn well. I can do anything if you are around without any hitch. You are my greatest strength, Vaani! I don't feel you are anyone different, I feel you are part of me." I just looked at the sky above and sighed, 'Why God!' is what I wanted to scream. The winds were intensifying, I could feel them on my face and I could hear them ringing in my ear. I felt like nature was empathizing with me. "If I mean so much to you then why didn't you marry me, Akash?" I sighed again. "People don't say wrong things about me for no reason, Vaani. I did have a past which was terrible. A few years back from now someone I really liked didn't stand up for me when the serious wedding talks started despite the promises that we would stick with each other. Losing her was painful but worse was that I lost a very good friend as well. I see a very special person in you and I didn't want to lose you and this bond ever. Moreover something else which I have learnt over the years is that wedding is not just about us, it's about many other relations which simultaneously become a part of our lives. I have seen so many people losing their special connection after they are married, no matter how much they try to be the same they end up being a forced routine for the other. Dependence and expectation slowly creep in and spoils everything. I don't mean to say weddings don't work but I just feel it's a different bond all together and I didn't want it at the cost of losing someone as special as you in my life. Besides this, my family has some bad scars associated with weddings in culture outside ours. So despite the fact that I liked you a lot I could never think beyond a certain point. That is why I could never promise anything to you. We will be the same old buddies; we will joke, laugh and be with each other." I was blank! How could he assume everything on my behalf! "You could have told me once, Akash. You knew I would have stood up, you knew I would have given it my best to keep it the same, you knew I could mend things in the family as well." "It's all very complicated, trust me. You would have been just nowhere with me, you are a girl you need to settle at the right time. I really feel Sahil is very good for you, you will be just fine. Anyways, leave it. There is no point in discussing all this now. I have to keep my parents happy and because they are getting older and also a little impatient about me getting married, I will have to marry sometime soon. If we have that special connection which we have always felt then trust me our bond won't go anywhere." I don't know whether he was right or wrong. But how difficult would it be for me, I thought, to change the role that I played in his life and still stick around, and still be the same. If he always wanted me to be just friends then why did he get so close to me? Why did he get physically involved with me? How could he think I won't get affected and would just move on? Probably he did so, because he was updated about the latest trends of relationships. Because that's how it was in the modern love relations. In the modern love relations, there is no connection between getting attached to one another and getting married to one another. In modern love relation, everyone is super strong; they feel they can come out of any phase whenever they want to. In modern day romance individuals are like flexible pieces of puzzles that keep playing around. "I always wanted to take you on a world tour. Meet me when you are forty-five, let's fulfill our social duties and obligations by then. At forty-five we will roam the world together and then I will tell you more on how and what I feel about you." Forty-five was far. I was turning thirty and forty-five was another fifteen years later. His words sounded like a small kid again, it reminded me of Shivani's son who once told me in all his innocence that he will gift me an airplane when he will become a big boy. Even Akash sounded equally innocent and equally concerned, I didn't know then about the changes that would have followed for the next fifteen years in both of our lives but all I did at that point in time was hoped that such a day would surely come when we would be the same again, probably all that I wanted to do from that point onwards was wait till I turned forty-five.

Two days later from then I finally departed to Lucknow where Sahil was, to begin a new life altogether; Akash dropped me to the airport in the early morning hours, it was a quiet drive with the least of conversation from either of us and a very painful parting. While on my way back I thought how could he assume that it was all complicated and how could he just assume that I would have been nowhere with him, he could have spoken everything clearly about his past, about all the hitches he had just once and maybe things would have turned the other way round. But I had to console myself somehow. I had to justify the wrong again to feel better, and thus I ended up thinking that sometimes we can't explain certain things about people with whom we cross paths when they are in the middle of their journey for life, when we haven't been with them or seen them in the hardships that they may have had, when we haven't really walked in their shoes since the beginning of their journey. Sometimes perhaps there might be a deeper reason existing for the smaller things that we see on the outside and sometimes perhaps there might be a mystery which the heaven holds for any two people who meet, fall in love but never unite.

Sahil received me very warmly at the airport and showed me everything on our way very enthusiastically. We were about to begin a brand new life and he was excited about it. I wished I could be like him, I wished I could undo the changes that had taken place in me and my life, I wished I could undo Akash from my life. Imagine a quiet jungle where everything is in harmony and every work is in order, the routine is fixed and the works are divided! What happens if there is a fire in the jungle one fine day? The order is gone and the base is shaken, the place is devastated and the jungle just strives to be the same again! The fire comes and goes, it doesn't repair or look back at the jungle or the damage it did, it's the jungle alone hoping to recover and be the same as it was one day. Akash was the fire in my balanced life!

CHAPTER 33

Ever since I had moved with Sahil after my wedding, I had kept myself strong and was trying my best to live in the moment, but I don't know what broke my inhibition that night which made me so weak that I failed to restrict Akash from entering my thoughts again. Yes I did have some struggles, yes I did have a lot of adjustments to make, but that was not an excuse for mingling my past with my present. Once the long-suppressed inhibition was gone, everything around seemed much more difficult than it was. I had started arguing with Sahil on every point, I did not want to adjust to anything, I did not want to be loved, and I did not want to even attempt to be happy. The irony of the whole thing was that this outer projection of a stubborn me was totally opposite to the broken and depressed inner me. At times, when all alone, I used to curl up in any corner of my house and cry for hours together; I used to get irritated at every small thing right from someone not answering my call, to times when I was unable to find my hairpin. Once after having faced rejection from a job I rushed to my house, locked myself up and screamed, "Take me from here Akash, save me please" I banged the floor and pushed the wall, I did all weird things to feel better, I screamed more and cried louder because I knew I won't be heard..I got relieved only once my tears dried up, after which I got up in a jerk, changed my clothes and went out with a face as though I was one of the happiest person alive! I and Akash were not in touch, we did not dare to be in touch, but I was unable to take him out of my thoughts. I used to narrate all my insecurities to Manav almost every day, until one day, when even he got married and busy in his life. It was indeed a big fat Indian wedding, he was very happy to have found a life partner, and I was equally happy for him. "Look at them and learn, people do have happy weddings," I said to myself that day, but unfortunately every voice failed to enter my ears including my own voice. Things became worse however after I lost Manav's telephonic support, the frequency of my small little attacks increased, where I got agitated and sad about everything happening in my life, where I failed to have any control over myself and all I could do was cry out loud, and feel helpless till I got tired. The worst was that I Vaani, who was once too proud to be my true self, could see all such astonishing changes in myself but was unable to control or do anything about it. Shivani had told me that Akash got married and settled in Australia. There I was, drowned in memories, struggling to stay happy, irritable and tortured, and there he must have been miles away from me I thought, making someone else smile! I had to move on, I had to accept my past as a mistake, misfortune or anything and I had to move on. But how?

I followed a fixed routine every day, and unable to find a stable job I had started working as a consultant in a few clinics around me which kept me little busy. While I was going out to work on one such day I saw Sahil's lunch-box lying on the table, "not again Sahil!" I said to myself, he had this habit of rushing out to work and forgetting something or the other in the house almost every day. Since his hospital was on my way, I decided to drive and drop the lunch at his workplace and then head for mine own. The hospital where he worked was huge; even though I had been there quite a few times I always had some struggle to find his chamber, and once again like every time I could see all the other departments but not his "Hmm...Cardiology Anesthesia, Emergency medicine, Psychiatry..." while I was looking around my eyes caught hold of Psychiatry for some reason. For a moment I stood in front of the corridor which led to the Psychiatrists chamber, where I saw a boy who must have been in his late twenties shouting at someone who appeared to be his mother. "I will not, I will not, I will not!" he said and pushed her hard; while from beside me passed an old lady who was sobbing and muttering something under her breath. I looked at them and I could see a flash of my own self, I felt an urge to see the psychiatrist. I froze there for a few minutes, and with great difficulty, I tried moving towards the doctor's chamber. "How can I need this consultation? I have been such a strong person. I have survived everything that I have faced. No, of course, I don't need any counselling, any medications" said one voice inside me, which was interfered by the other voice which immediately argued and said, "I have to meet the doctor, I have to tell him how I feel, I want to sit next to him and cry. He has never known me, he won't judge me, and he won't say that I have become weak and dependent." I could feel tremors as I walked ahead, all of a sudden a happy Vaani flashed in front of me; Vaani who was hard-working and energetic, Vaani who was spontaneous and fun-loving, Vaani who was caring and flirtatious. I think the trouble that I faced in moving towards that chamber was because the taboos and social stigmas associated in our society to any form of mental illness are way too many. Even though I just wanted to talk to the doctor about my present state I could see the number of fingers that would have been raised on me if anyone came to know about this. Lost in my own world I stood there till someone tapped on my shoulder from behind, "Hey Vaani! Lost your way again I guess?" it was one of Sahil's colleague who recognized me and laughed. I too pretended to have lost my way and giggled, he guided me the way for Sahil's chamber, I thanked him, smiled once again and went ahead to give him the lunch-box.

To pretend is such a funny two-sided sword I thought; it does protect your emotions and saves you momentarily, but in the long run, it ends up killing you gradually.

CHAPTER 34

"How are you doing, Vaani, and how about your anniversary plans this year?" Asked my mother over the phone. She was someone who used to constantly remind me of the smaller and bigger things and dates. It did not even occur to me that my wedding anniversary was approaching in the next seven days. "Sixth wedding anniversary!" I said to myself. "Yes it's not sixtieth it's just sixth. You are still a young couple, plan a good holiday," she continued. "But I don't feel like going on a holiday mom. I just don't feel like doing anything at all. I feel weird all the time, release me from this cage." I wanted to say, but I preferred to keep quiet. Because the last time that I tried telling her that, she gave me a lesson on how things in our society were, how divorce could lead to a lot of bad consequences, and how I will have to end up staying alone etc. How I wish I could scream and tell her, that I was killing myself every day and I was just not able to survive anything around me, but, unfortunately even she was blind to my state of mind.

It was a long day for me because I had no call for consultations. Sahil came back from work a little earlier than usual. As a routine, I made some tea for us and we sat together. He took the newspaper and started flipping through the pages. "So, you didn't go anywhere today?" He said while continuing to look at the newspaper. "No I didn't. How was your day?" I asked him. "Hectic as usual, but somehow we winded up a little early. Oh! Sachin in retiring from one-day matches, this is so sad, cricket won't be as good anymore!" He seemed to be engrossed in the news. I used to get a little annoyed at this previously but that's the way he usually had the conversations, he rather multi-tasked. I had a lot to talk, but I wanted to be heard, not technically but with complete devotion. I wanted someone to sit with me, look at me and understand me. Sahil's phone rang. It was from his ward. "Yes I had written the blood investigations, and please tell the patients to give my reference so that they can get some discount from the pathology." He was totally occupied in his work and was packed with things to do. I had a sense of discomfort. I wanted to talk to him, but how, I thought. He took his teacup to the kitchen, kept it, and then finally sat on his study table to read something. He didn't notice that I was around him and I was looking for an opportunity to talk to him. "He is my husband, he has always been a good friend, talk to him," I said to myself and went ahead, I kept my hand on his shoulder from behind, he turned back and looked at me. "I want to talk to you, Sahil," I said gathering some strength. "Yes, tell me," he said while still sitting on his study chair. "I don't want to tell you anything Sahil. I want to talk to you, and I want some time of yours. Not here. Not with your phones ringing, not with you doing something else," my eyes had welled up. Understanding the need and seriousness of that moment Sahil stood up. We sat on the dining table, he looked at me straight in my eyes, "Go ahead, Vaani. I am listening," he said.

I did have some such conversations with him previously as well, but this one was a lot more different. I had no idea of what I wanted to say, and I had no idea that in that discomfort I would say things which I wouldn't have told him otherwise. "Sahil you are a nice man. You are completely devoted towards your work and your patients. You do your duties well, and I do have bread in the house on time, and all the time. But..." I paused and cleared my throat while I was actually clearing my thoughts. "But, have you ever tried to go deep and see what is actually going on inside me?" I continued, "Whether I am as happy as I should be? Do you have any idea, what I do when I am all alone in the house, which is more than many-a-times I suppose? I have tried talking to you about little things previously as well, but it's still the same. I had so many dreams and ambitions, I had thought so differently about my life." "Yes, we have spoken about this previously, Vaani. You do have consultations now which you did not have previously, things are much better than what it was when this all began," he attempted to assure me. "Consultations are not as regular and also they do not let me work the way I want to," I said. "But Vaani I am taking care of the bills right, did I ever complain?" "Bills! Come on Sahil. It's not about making the payments on time. We have been able to do nothing close to what we wanted to do because we are constantly solving our own issues. At least I have done nothing close to what I wanted to do and you too know that." In the struggle that I was going through I had once told Sahil that I wanted to study further about healthcare management. I had exchanged a few e-mails with a university in Berlin which even assured me of a good placement after the course, but then again the in-laws issues, *you can't stay away from your husband* issues had cropped up and that topic had died. "Yes, I know that you wanted to study further and you always wanted to venture somewhere else for some time, but you know I can't do that. I am sorry again, but I am bound to this place. And we did try planning out for the service-oriented healthcare center together. But I don't think we can do it with so many personal clutters, at least for a few more years." Sahil and I did not have a child, it was by a common consent. Because we fought most of the times, and we were struggling with our own lives, we did not want to influence a naïve life like this. Some people suggested us to have one so that things may improve and take a new turn. But we knew what our inhibitions and problems were, so, fortunately, we both had given a deaf ear to what everyone else said. "Every nook and corner of the house has heard me scream, has heard me cry, has been a victim of the little bombarding which I do when you are away," I was beginning to open up more, "I cry loudly and I talk to myself. I shout out loud and I ask the heaven above, that what was my mistake, why am I facing all this, why am I not able to be the Vaani which you had loved, but I fail to get an answer," I was sobbing by now. "I did change, but I did not want to, the circumstances had taken over me back then, and the circumstances have taken over me now again. I don't know if it's my work, or my loneliness, if it's my hallucinations or the reality if it's you or still Akash. I DON'T KNOW WHAT IS BOTHERING ME SAHIL!" I screamed and broke down. Sahil was looking straight at me, no newspaper, no books, not even a blink; he was just looking at me. "I am not sure if I should apologize to you for being blind and busy over these years, or console you at this moment or if I should cry with you, or shout at you for having held so many things back in your heart for so long. Maybe because you have always come across as so strong and independent, I thought that you were fine. I never realized the pain and loneliness which you may have been going through over these years. Akash surely is somewhere in your mind right now. But there is a lot more which has added on and brought you to the present state, and even I am responsible for it," his voice was stern and he continued, "I have not been able to give you time, and neither have I been able to help you in your ventures, but even I was helpless and I still am. My workplace is here and I am bound to my family. As far Akash is concerned I feel it was his mistake for not having stood up for you. No matter how many reasons he may have quoted, the younger generation romance is like that, Vaani. People pretend to be carefree and detached, whereas in reality they are constantly affected by it and they don't even realize it until they get completely eaten up from within and until things start falling apart. Don't suppress your thoughts about the past. Just let it free, and you will be all good at least in that aspect. And as far as I am concerned, Vaani..." he held my hand, "I have never bothered about your past and I have loved you with all my heart. But still I have been responsible for your pain in some way today. I did not realize, but I kept you bound all these years. I can't see you suffocate more. I want you to do all those things which you have wanted to do. I want you to be free from my cultural obligations. I will take a stand for you, live your life Vaani, and if you are happy, I will be happy. Apply for a job abroad, let us go our separate ways for some time. Let us go back to our best selves again and be the two same mature teenagers, with a will to do good and with the energy to achieve anything." I hugged him tightly and sobbed. After ages together I felt I was understood. I felt I was heard, I felt I had my friend back. I felt light, very light. Yes I did not need any medication or any counseling. All I needed was some courage to open up, and all I needed was someone of my own who could understand me and support me without getting judgmental about me. Sahil and I hadn't been good as husband and wife because of the burdens of expectations which I had from him. But I was fortunate to have found this sense of empathy in him. When everyone else near me failed to support me, he did, when everyone else near me found it difficult to break the cultural ties, he did, when everyone else failed to identify my state of mind and my need, he did.

I applied for Masters In healthcare Administration in Berlin, and with a green tick in all their criteria I managed to get an admission in the university. Sahil and I parted on a happy note. We did have to face some friction from our families, because depression is really hard to be understood by most of the people, and specifically when the girl has been trained in a part of medical sciences herself, nobody expects her to face it. If the world realized that any mental illness had nothing to do with the profession, the status, the gender and the age then I may have opened up earlier about it and I could have saved a few years of my life. Nevertheless, our families supported us at last, and we moved away for our works. A new life was awaiting us.

CHAPTER 35

Immediately after the course got over I got hired by a reputed hospital in Dubai as an Assistant medical superintendent. I was leading a new and independent life. Manav was still my buddy and Akash was still a visitor of my mind and heart but luckily after Sahil's lecture I never tried to suppress my past and rather made peace with it. So it never bothered me much. It just made me smile. Over those years things improved professionally for Sahil as well. By taking the decision to move away from each other for a couple of years we had started bonding more with each other. We kept meeting each other often, we were very much like the same old friends that we were once upon a time. In one of my visits to India we visited an orphanage. It was my birthday that day and we wanted to spend some time with the children there and donate some things from our side. Doing something for the homeless little children gave us a lot of satisfaction. The day we visited, someone had dropped a newborn girl child there. I looked at her and she looked back at me with sheer innocence. She was pure and unaffected by anything in this world, she would have become the way she would have been groomed. "I would groom her," I told Sahil, "I will prepare her to face the world and stay unaffected by it at the same time. Let's adopt her." Sahil was more than happy with my decision. We went to the owner and fulfilled the formalities of adoption; Aradhna is what we named her.

CHAPTER 36

Aradhna and I stayed together in Dubai. We celebrated our birthday on the same day; it was her seventh and my forty-fifth that day. I was almost an hour late from work, I told my driver to rush as fast as he could, the bakery guy must be at the door already I was getting tensed. The moment I reached my house I found him waiting. I am glad I was on time else he would have gone back I thought. I stood at the door and opened my purse in a rush. I wanted to receive the cake and keep it before Aradhna came back with her nanny from her friend's place; I wanted to surprise her with her favorite Minion-shaped cake. In that moment of rush I couldn't find my wallet, I started digging my purse, every other thing came out of it except any Dirhams. I accidentally took out my old wallet, and dropped it on the floor. "Oops sorry! That's the old one," I looked at the delivery boy with embarrassed eyes. Thankfully I finally found some money to settle his bills, I took the cake, kept it aside, and started putting the spill overs back in my purse. As I picked up my old wallet the papers and other things in it fell on the floor; while I was keeping them back I picked up a piece of paper. I knew this paper, it was a little love note which Sahil had given me years ago, "*....if I'm not mad then certainly I am In love with you*" was the last line which was highlighted by him; on that note I had wrapped a half burnt cigarette and for a second I could smell Akash in it. I had kept it safe in my wallet and never looked at it again until today. I knew Aradhana would have come anytime soon, but all my hurry disappeared. I couldn't get up. I just sat there on the floor with the half burnt cigarette and the little love note and thought how my life had changed so much over a period of years, in fact how much I had changed my life over a period of years, and how the Vaani who received these two was so different from the one who sat with them now. But I was proud that despite the many changes that had happened in my life, I had stayed strong and survived every phase with hope.

My phone was constantly beeping; there were birthday messages from many friends and colleagues, I was glad that they remembered, I glanced through the notifications from my main screen, Racheal, Aftab, Home, Aruna aunty, Shivani, Dr. Akash! "What, who?" I said to myself in surprise. I hadn't heard from him for years now and he had no clue where I was. How could it be him. I opened the message and realized that it was an e-mail; my e-mail id was still the same and he had it. I opened it and it read as follows:

"Hey, Beautiful!

Many happy returns of the day! How is Dubai treating you? Surprised! How do I know where you are? Well, I have always kept a track on you through some common old colleagues of ours. I have been in Australia and I have been just fine. I have lived all my dreams, I have done almost everything that I always wanted to. I have worked to the maximum of my capability. My wedding didn't work. I never got along with anyone the way I got along with you. You were just perfect Vaani, with you I could be truly carefree and myself. I have many friends here and my family keeps visiting me every now and then, but in the midst of all that I have had, I have always missed you. You could never be replaced. Back then I was at fault. I don't know how I could even let you go. I don't know what all you must have gone through in all these years and I don't know how to even apologize to you for the emotional turmoil that you may have faced because of me. I was so mature and yet so immature. It was my fault to get ahead in the relationship with you, despite knowing that I couldn't stay with you, despite knowing that I couldn't take a stand for you. Life has taught me a lot of lessons.

By the way next week I will be in your city, I know we shouldn't remind ladies about their age but I hope you noticed that you turned forty-five today. Back then I made a promise to get back to you when you turn forty-five. I couldn't afford to break this promise, Vaani. I want to make up for everything I did by spending the rest of my life with you. Will you marry me? And by the way there is one way in which I am still the same, I am the same impatient Akash. So I didn't wait for your "yes" before booking my tickets, I know for me it has always been a "yes, of course" from Vaani. I will be there next week. I am eager and I am counting days.

P.S: See you soonest and do mail me your address

Akash"

While I was smiling and lost in my own thoughts, my phone rang and it was Sahil who had called. "Thank you for your wishes!" I said as soon as I answered. "Madam," he said, "thank me later, open the door first, I have been ringing the bell since so long, where are you?" "Oops," I rushed to open the door, and found Sahil standing there with a big bouquet and a folder in his hand and backpack on his back. "Surprised?" He raised his eyebrow. "Pleasantly," I said and smiled. "So let me surprise you a little more Mrs. Vaani." He opened the folder which he was holding in his hand. Here is our dream project in black and white; it's a service-oriented multi-specialty children's hospital to cater the needs of the thousands of children who don't survive because of their poor financial state. I have already purchased the major machinery and finished the construction of dedicated floors for various treatments, and by the way I have dedicated a floor to the children's dental treatment as well. I am getting it registered next month and we will begin it full-fledged in a maximum of two months time. And yes, he took out another file, "I have purchased a beautiful little villa in one of the best township in the city, which now needs to be furnished in our own style. So Mrs. Vaani," he bent on his knees, and gave me his hand, "can I have the honor to have someone as amazing and talented as you to be the administrator of our dream project and our dream home?" This time even his eyes had welled up. "Of course," I said immediately, and bent down and looked at him, in that moment of mixed emotions we kissed, and yes we kissed like we had never kissed before. There were no other thoughts, no other interferences, no misunderstandings and no expectations. It was just me with my man who probably waited for this moment ever since the day he had given me the little love note. "Wait!" I suddenly withdrew myself from him, "Hey, all good?" he asked. "Hmm, ya give me a minute. I just remembered I left something unfinished." I opened my phone and typed my smallest ever reply to Akash, "Cancel your tickets. Good luck with your life." They say, "Time and tide wait for none" and I am sure Akash would have learnt yet another lesson with this e-mail of mine. The slow and steady romance had persisted and stayed, while the hasty and electrifying romance had come and vanished.

There are these moments when your tears and your smile confuse you when you don't know whether to get up and dance or put your head down and cry, this was one such moment for me. In that one moment I found myself back, I found my balance back, I felt rich, I felt complete, and I felt at peace. With a strange comfort on my face after years together I got up and decorated my house to the best of my capabilities, Aradhna would have been here any time now and it was time to celebrate; I had turned forty-five today and yes it was time to celebrate.

EPILOGUE

A few years ahead…

Life truly takes many unexpected turns, where once Vaani was waiting to unite with Akash on her forty-fifth birthday she finally fell in love with Sahil. Vaani and Sahil worked hard to reach out to the unreached segments of their native state to provide healthcare lessons and vaccinations. They managed to provide care to a vast population of children through their hospital. With the work that they did within no time they were joined by many other enthusiastic healthcare providers as well.

In the present day, Sahil is still as busy but the good thing is that now Vaani is busier. She is more than happy to look after the administration of the entire hospital besides which she runs the floor dedicated to children's dental health as well. But they both make sure that their family has atleast one meal together. They don't hold little problems and complaints in their hearts anymore; they talk about them, sort them and finish them.

Akash chose to settle in Australia. He says he loves the culture of Melbourne city and is happy to fly to India on and off. His parents retired from work and have moved him now. He tried contacting Vaani after their last e-mail but as Vaani said, time had moved on in a very different way so he never heard back from her. He chose not to marry again but is settled well with his work. How well? Well, he never opened up about that.

Aradhna is growing up to be an enthusiastic photographer, and Vaani is leaving no stone unturned in doing everything to make her follow her passion.

Manav ended up joining a renowned institute and is a very popular professor now. He didn't bag any gold medals himself but is now the reason behind the gold medals of many young Dental graduates.

They all moved ahead in their lives and are doing fairly well to themselves but they could have definitely saved a few years if they knew the importance of communication well. They all realized that life comprised of a much bigger picture than what we always see, that life was all about learning from one's mistakes and moving on without stopping. They realized that human relations are very precious and have to be preserved, and nurtured and should not be left to the mercy of time.

Cigarette smoking is injurious to health.